WILD RIDE
TO HEAVEN

WILD RIDE
TO HEAVEN

By Leander Watts

Houghton Mifflin Company
Boston 2003

www.houghtonmifflinbooks.com

The text of this book is set in 11-point Janson

Library of Congress Cataloging-in-Publication Data
Watts, Leander.
Wild ride to heaven / Leander Watts.
p. cm.
Summary: A girl with one green eye and the other milky is sold by her
drunken father into servitude to two brutish brothers from her
poverty-stricken pioneer village, downriver from Lake Ontario.
ISBN 0-618-26805-7
[1. Disfigured persons—Fiction. 2. Fathers and daughters—Fiction. 3.
Sex role—Fiction. 4. Albinos and albinism—Fiction. 5. Frontier and
pioneer life—Fiction. 6. Brothers—Fiction.] I. Title.
PZ7.W339 Wi 2003
[Fic]—dc21

Manufactured in the United States of America
QUM 10 9 8 7 6 5 4 3 2 1

Chapter 1

THO HE WAS POOR AS THE DIRT, MY PA GAVE ME THREE gifts more costly than any jewels.

The first is my name, that being Hannah Renner.

The second gift was reading and writing. The girls I knew got hardly a few days of the alphabet before they were sent back to spinning and cooking and sewing. But my pa, filthy with charcoal dust and more often than not under the sway of whiskey and other ardent spirits, still made sure I had a slate to practice my writing on when I was little, and then paper and ink and quill when I got older. There were always books and newspapers around, and he never once told me to put them down and get back to work.

The third gift may not seem a gift at all. But it's my queerly mismatched eyes. Some folks have called them a curse and others a blessing, and indeed I think they were both, as you shall see.

Folks said that when my eyes were closed, I had a pretty face. Sleeping, or resting in the sunshine listening to the bright buzz of the honeybees, my face was a pleasure to behold.

But folks looked away when I opened my eyes, for the left one is as pale as nearly frozen milk, and the right one is a deep sea green. At least that's what Pa would say, as I'd never glimpsed the ocean nor even Lake Ontario, fifty miles up the river from where we lived.

My eyes are strange, but my vision is just fine. Indeed, some old gossips in Black Stick said I could see better because of my strange eyes. Still, the look of them, like a moonstone and a polished jade side by side in the same setting, made folks afraid.

Chapter 2

MY FRIEND PHOEBE CALE WAS ALREADY PUTTING AWAY bits of linen and even a few spoons in a box she said would be replaced by a hope chest on her fourteenth birthday. And Jane Reed, who had always been the kindest of the town girls, was spending far more time of late primping and combing her hair and gazing into the looking glass.

But I knew that I must live my life in a different way from other girls. Besides living a far piece from town and having a half-crazed pa, I had no sisters nor ma to speak of.

I suppose even if my eyes weren't so strange — and when I was little how I prayed that God would make them the same so that folks would stop staring and murmuring — my life would not have run on a normal path. Phoebe and Jane and Melanie Reed knew exactly the road their lives would go down: catching the eyes of the boys, courting, marriage, and children. For me that road was not just blocked but heaped up with boulders. One strange-eyed girl was bad enough. Certainly no young man would want to start a whole brood of them.

Not that boys were much on my mind. From what I saw of them on my trips into Black Stick, they weren't half as bright as girls and twice as clumsy. Mostly they talked too loud and spat too much tobacco juice. Generally, they got better schooling than girls, so they should have known better. But reciting the names of the emperors of Rome or the capitals of all the twenty-six United States didn't make them any more civil to be around. Pa taught me to read and write. So I didn't see much point in sitting on hard benches listening to Mr. Vance drone on.

Most everybody seemed to think it was a great advantage being a boy. Boys could smoke cigars. But I found that to be a noxious thing. Folks didn't seem to mind much if boys got into the keg now and then. Of drinking ardent spirits, however, I'd already seen enough to last me a lifetime. My pa wasted too much money on whiskey and cider and the occasional jug of cherry bounce. From his stumbling and snoring and disorderly ways, I was sure I wanted no part in getting drunk.

The only advantages I could see then to being a boy was the cursing and the guns. And my pa let me have a pretty free rein with both of those. He let me take the fowling piece out into the woods to scrounge up some meat, rabbit or squirrel mostly, when there was nothing else to eat. I'd gotten to be a pretty fair shot, tho it troubled me at times to bear aim on little beasts that had done me no harm nor never would.

And I had learned some bitter foul oaths from Pa. He said he heard them off of canal men, and if the Reverend Mr. Yates was telling true, most of them had monstrous vulgar tongues. But if no one was around to hear my curses, they didn't seem to do any harm or good. When you live in a place like Black Stick, little things like curses don't seem to fret anybody the way they would in a real town.

I say we lived in Black Stick, but really that was just the closest village. And it was a good nine miles away along a winding, rutted path barely wide enough for my pa's wagon. Even compared to Little Sion, the next town up the river, there wasn't much to Black Stick. Folks called it a village, tho it was hardly a crossroad hamlet: a general store, a meetinghouse (which was for both school and Sunday service), and a dozen other buildings.

Pa carted his rustling sooty loads of charcoal into Black Stick, and usually I went along. Most times, Mr. Harmon would make trade for Pa's charcoal and then send it up farther north. Some of it went to the smithy in Little Sion and some even farther, to the manufactures at Rochester, where the Grand Erie Canal crossed over the Genesee River. At times, too, he'd make barter for the wild honey I might gather. We'd get brown sugar, gunpowder, salt, pickled fish, coffee, and tea. Once in a while, when Pa was happy with too much spirits, he'd let me trade my wares for indigo dye or red ribbon, and once a stretch of fine calico. I sewed a dress of that material which none of the girls in town could boast better of. This, of course, set some evil tongues wagging. "What makes her think she can wear such a fine frock?" old Mrs. Reed had said, not exactly behind my back. Another nodded and said in not quite a whisper, "Such a pretty girl but for those dreadful eyes. Sins of the father meted out to the child."

And then I heard two boys talking about a farmer up at Little Sion who had a lamb born with strange, mismatched eyes. "He killed the lamb quick and threw it out in the woods for the wolves," the first boy had said. "Had a curse on it, and if you ate the flesh or wore cloth wove from the wool, the curse would take onto you like poison."

Both the boys looked at me as I passed. They were afraid of me. But they were drawn, too, as Pa would say, like hawkmoths to a bright candle flame.

Nobody had ever said within my hearing that I should be killed like that lamb and tossed away for the ravening beasts to devour. But I wouldn't have been surprised if some of the folks in Black Stick had dwelt on such thoughts now and again.

Chapter 3

THE DAY WHEN THE TWO BARROW BROTHERS CAME TO our cabin asking for my pa, I knew it could only mean bad tidings.

My pa'd much as sooner been all by himself, reading or working on some new backward and forward idea. When he brought folks home it meant he owed them money and wanted to wriggle out of the debt. Sometimes he'd try to sweet-talk them, but that didn't work very often. Other times I think he wanted to show them how dirt-poor we were and how there wasn't hardly anything there to repossess. Once in a while I think he wanted to show them his strange-eyed daughter and maybe scare them that I'd do some kind of witchery mischief on them. Most times, however, he had creditors come out because he was trying to waste time until he could reckon out another plan.

The Barrows were great hulking men, low in the forehead

and thick in the arms. You could have cut two of my pa out of each one, with enough left over to scrape together a girl my size. So together they were like a great wall blocking out the sun.

I'd seen them only twice or thrice before. They owned a big piece of land a few miles farther past our place. It was between nowhere and no place in particular, so I imagine they saw even fewer folks than we did. They didn't go to Sunday meeting. I'd never heard Pa talk about them drinking with the other men. They had no wives or children, so there wasn't any cause for me crossing their paths.

But there they were on my doorstep, towering as big as a pair of thunderclouds. Because of their size and their sullen hulking ways, I thought of them as being Pa's age. But as I was to learn, they weren't barely ten years older than me.

Their arms seemed as big around as tree stumps. Their heads were close cropped, raggedy, as if they had cut each other's hair with broken crockery. One brother was missing a finger. The other had a bite-size piece taken out of his ear.

They had to lean over to come inside the shanty, which I did not say they should do. They hunched down, came in, and took up half the room.

One was called Leon, and the other Noel. Later, when I told my pa about the visit, he remarked that the names were much out of the ordinary. "One backward is the other forward. Noel-Leon." He got a serious look on his face. "It's like your name, Hannah. Backward and forward it's the same."

The brothers looked around our place. But they were regarding me too, looking closely. "She doesn't appear as I expected," one said in a rumbling, far-off thunder voice. "Bit of a surprise."

"You're saying true. Close her eyes and she's half fair to look upon." They talked as tho I wasn't there or was just a three-legged stool or a young porker they were considering to buy.

"Lives like a savage tho," one said. "Place is hardly fit for a brood of Seneca."

It's true that my pa could not afford much in the way of luxuries. Every extra penny went to buying some new book that weighed almost as much as me. He'd wait for months sometimes to get ahold of a new book. They'd come by the mail stage to Little Sion, and then somebody would haul the mail to Black Stick and Pa'd trek in there as soon as he heard Mr. Harmon had it waiting for him at the store. So the cabin had not much in the way of niceties. There were certainly times I wished we had real panes of glass for the windows and not oiled paper. I would have liked to sleep on fine linens and serve tea from a proper pot. But if I had to choose between those or being able to read and write, there was no question which I'd take.

The brothers came in farther, inspecting, then backed out. For such big men, they didn't move clumsy, but slow and almost dreamlike. They'd learned, I suppose, not to go too fast. Big men have to, or they topple everything in a house.

Outside, I joined them and closed the door tight behind me.

"My pa's not here right now, as you can plain see. He's out tending the ricks."

Noel nodded. He was the older one, a little bigger and heavier too, the one with the missing finger. "We know that. We're just here to see the place."

"And you," Leon added. "And you, girl."

"What for do you want to see me?" I asked. "You never heard of me before nor I of you except a few words." I didn't like this one little jot. Most times there was no reason to be vexed about being alone. In fact, I liked fending for myself. But this day, I wished my pa was there to send these men on their way.

"We heard plenty," Noel said. "Your pa can be a talker when he gets a hooker or two of cider into his gut. Then he talks and talks till you can hardly shut him up."

"What did he say?" I asked, but I could already imagine it, hear all the boasting he'd do on me. One time he told a traveling preacher that I could read the Bible better than any girl or woman in the whole of the Genesee Valley. So the preacher rode out to our place and stayed three days while I read for him and showed that not any of the old book names, from Adoniram to Ziporah, were too hard for me to say clear and loud. He talked about God and salvation and Heaven, and it surprised me that even my pa stayed around and listened.

But the Barrow brothers were no preacher men. I doubt they'd ever sat through one whole sermon or hymn. They'd come not to hear me read but to look me over and up and down.

"He told us you had a pretty voice for singing."

Pa got into trouble with his talking, but he never told lies. It was a true fact that I could carry a tune and even make fair harmonies on top if someone else kept the melody strong.

"He called you his nightingale," Noel said.

"When I was little, that was his name for me. But now I'm just Hannah."

"We came because your pa told us how you can work hard and how you're fair to behold if we don't mind the eyes."

"And how you can sing like an angel from the heavenly choir," his brother added, quieter, not so brash as the other one.

"That may be," I said. "But you got to come back another time when Pa's around. I think you'd better leave now." My saying this surprised the brothers, and me too. I wasn't less hospitable than anyone else around, but being alone with the brothers seemed a wrong thing. "I don't like you," I said quiet. "You'll have to come back when Pa's here."

"She don't like us, brother," Noel said. "Little Miss Nightingale don't like us."

"She'll have to learn to like us, I guess," Leon said. "She'll have to learn, and mighty fast."

With that, they lumbered off down the trail like two oak trees come to life. I stood by the door until they were gone, a sentry standing guard. When they disappeared around the bend, I set off the opposite way to tell my pa.

Chapter 4

I RAN ALL THE WAY TO THE FIRE YARD. IT WAS MORE than a mile to the nearest one. Pa had been cutting and burning wood since I was little, and he'd cleared quite a few acres.

It was a misty day, and smoke hung in long swaths overhead. I suppose a sawyer's daughter would always think of her pa as smelling of cut wood. And a tanner's girl would forever recall her father when she smelt leather and hides. For me, smoke and my pa would always go together. Smoke and soot and ash.

He'd been out minding this rick for a few days now. It usually took about two weeks for the great pile of sawn logs to smolder down to charcoal. He'd come back to the shanty once a day for me to give him some food, but usually he slept out in one of the little lean-to hovels to keep a good eye on the fires and make sure they didn't go out of control.

There was a huge big mound of earth with little holes for

the smoke to come out. Usually he made the mounds the shape of a beehive. Inside, instead of honey and comb and wax, however, were a dozen or so cords of wood, all cut about four feet in length. He'd spend a few weeks chopping and stacking, and then shovel up a layer of earth over the whole thing, and when he thought the rick was all ready, he'd shove a few burning poles into the breather holes. For the pittance he got for his labors, ten or fifteen cents per bushel, it seemed an awful dreary amount of toil. But it did make him hard cash, which he could spend to buy more books.

I shouted out for him but got no reply. The fire yards are a sore ugly place. Black soot and ash blows all over. The earth is dug and torn up and fills with miry puddles after the rain. I looked into his little hut, but it was empty.

Again I hollered for him. My voice sounded more lonely there than if it had been echoing in the woods proper. The fingers of smoke twisted like ghosts who've been disturbed from their sleep. I called one more time, and it seemed as though the great mound of smoldering wood let out a low gasp. I knew that minding the intake of air and breathing out the smoke was a delicate art. My pa had got mighty skilled at adjusting the big piles. I'd spent some time out there keeping him company. But I'd never heard this hollow sucking-in sound.

I didn't want to go back to the cabin without first telling

him about the Barrow brothers' visit. There'd been a few times he needed to hide out for a week or two from creditors. I thought for sure the brothers were coming around to collect on a debt, and Pa'd need to make a plan.

A deep rumble came from inside the burning pile, then a plume of black smoke jetted out from one of the holes. It seemed the hole was getting bigger, tearing downward. I saw a little glow of embers inside.

So I grabbed up a shovel from by the shack and set to throwing earth over the growing hole.

"Here, give me that," I heard Pa say. He'd come from behind without my hearing a footstep. He grabbed the shovel and soon had the hole all tamped down proper. "Burning a little too hot," he said. But he didn't seem worried, and once he was there, tending, the strange gaspy rumbly sounds ceased.

"There were two men come out to the cabin," I said. "The Barrow brothers."

He frowned and scooped up a little clay with his shovel. "What they want?"

"That's what I come out here to ask you, Pa. They're peculiar men. Didn't say much but looked all around like there was something at the shanty they had a claim on."

Pa stabbed the shovel into the earth, hard and wrathy, like it was a spear and he was aiming for his enemy's heart.

"How much money do you owe them, Pa?"

"Not a penny, and that's the truth," he said.

"Then what for did they come around? That was no friendly visit just to give their greetings to the neighbors. They wanted something."

"I don't owe them not one cent."

I believed him. When he said "that's the truth," it always was. Still, I knew there was trouble brewing, and I feared Pa didn't know which direction it would come from.

Tho he had powerful arms from swinging the ax all day, Pa was not a big man. He was only a few inches taller than me, and I hadn't reached my full height yet. He was strong, and he knew words from his books that nobody in the whole county knew, and some wisdom had come to him with his years. But there were times when it seemed as if I was the grownup and he the child.

He stood sullen and quiet, not telling me what had gone on between him and the Barrows. With his head hung low, he might have been a schoolboy and me the mistress quizzing him.

"I heard Elim Sanders talking about some fellows down at Dansville who claimed they'd found real treasure. Gold or silver. They said it was an ancient horde, left behind by the people who lived here long before the Seneca came."

"Did Mr. Sanders see this treasure?"

Pa shook his head.

"Did Mr. Sanders know these men?"

"No. They were wayfarers looking to see what kind of land there was to be bought hereabouts."

"Pa, you tell me right now. What's this got to do with the Barrow brothers?"

"You know this charcoal burning is fierce hard work. And I got to go farther afield for the wood every year. I hardly get a dime for a bushel. I can't do this kind of work when I'm an old man."

"I told you, when I get bigger you can live with me, and I'll take care of you."

"A man's supposed to take care of himself, not depend on his little girl."

"I'll be all grown up then. That's the way it is, Pa. Look at old Mr. Townsend. He worked his farm for years, and now he lives with Jimmy and his new wife, and he doesn't have to plow nor sow nor reap no more."

"I want to be a rich man now. I want to sit by the fire and read my books and not have to cut and dig and burn and cart the charcoal like a slave."

"When I'm grown you can do that."

He wouldn't say more than that. He went back to minding the rick, inspecting the breather holes, and he wouldn't answer any more of my questions. I stayed out there at the fire yard for a while, but his silence was too much to bear after a while, and I went back to the cabin.

Chapter 5

I MADE UP A LITTLE MEAL FOR MYSELF, CORN BREAD and pork, which is what we ate most times. Then I sat for a while thinking, looking into the fire. I'd do that of an evening, watching the little tongues and fingers of fire playing in the hearth. I didn't believe in fairies and hobgoblins and the like, but looking into the fire, sitting there all by myself, sometimes I could almost convince myself that there were spirits around us. It just took a flint and steel for the spark and some good tinder to get the fire going, and out the little scarlet and golden flickering creatures came.

Or so it felt on a night like that.

I sat there in the chair that had been my ma's. "Her favorite spot in the whole world," Pa called it. I sat there and pondered on what had happened that day. He had some plan, that was sure. There was some scheme hatching, and the Barrow brothers were certainly part of it.

People in Black Stick thought of my pa as a lazy reprobate.

His trade, or so they said, consisted mostly of sitting and doing nothing. It's true that when the ricks were burning, he'd bide there in his little hut "to keep the fire company," as he put it. But to make the fire needed weeks of cutting wood first, snaking the logs down to the fire yard, and digging up small mountains of earth.

There's no question that our farmstead was not the best it could be. Our fields were often in a sorry state. Pa had no patience for plowing a straight furrow, and I wasn't strong enough. And it's true, our beasts often went untended. But he wasn't lazy. In fact, he was what I would call a searching man. Sometimes it was hunting in the woods, other times just sitting by the fire hearth. No matter what his hands were doing, his mind was searching.

People in Black Stick had never seen him in one of his concentrating moods, more intensified and hardworking than any honeybee searching out nectar flower after flower. His mind would turn and turn like a mill wheel in a steady spring draft, and I could almost hear the gears and shafts grinding inside his mind. Three whole days he once went, paging through my ma's Bible, muttering at times, jotting down notes, and cursing and laughing a little and saying "yes, yes, yes," and then drumming his fingers on the side of his head. He had the look of a frantic man who'd lost a precious treasure and thought he might find it in the pages of the book.

I suspected at that time he was searching in the Bible to

find some reason why Ma went off the way she did. But other times it didn't seem that his searching could have anything to do with that one thing, which we never talked about.

Another time, he spent a week with a willow wand, but he said he wasn't dousing for water. He paced back and forth outside in zigzag patterns, then in widening loops away from the cabin. He was talking to himself (or maybe to the spirits, as the folks in town whispered) and watching the wand's end for a little shake or tremble that said to look right there.

One time he brought whole bushels of oak leaves back to the shanty and inspected them one by one, tossing each with a disgusted sigh into the fire.

And later I found him on the riverbank in a place with thousands of pebbles shining bright in the sunlight. He was picking them up one at a time and holding them to the sun, and then flinging them into the river.

These kinds of fascinations came and went, but the one place where his search never stopped was in words. He hunted through words like you might search through all the stars in the wide night sky to find the one you could make a wish upon. He had books and almanacks. He had newspapers, tho these were often months out of date because Black Stick wasn't on the stagecoach lines. He had the Bible and songsters and old letters and legal papers. And he'd search through all the words and write them down, then turn them backward and forward, inside out, scribbling all the letters.

"Look here," he'd say. "'Live' backward is 'evil.' But if you stir the letters up you also get 'veil,' like what a bride wears, and 'vile' and 'Levi.' Wasn't he one of the old Bible book prophets?"

I'd have to nod and say "yes, Pa, that's true," and pretend that I understood what all his thinking was about.

One time I hadn't seen him for a few days when he burst into the shanty as excited as if he'd heard the angel Gabriel blowing the final trumpet. "Hannah!" he shouted. I'd been churning a long while and my arms ached, and I still had hours of work to do in the cornfield. But I put down the dasher and looked at his little scrap of paper. I don't remember exactly what he had there, but it was some word puzzle, letters going this way and that, arrows and circles. I suppose he thought it had some sort of magical power, a spell captured on paper. I think they call them amulets. He was all agitated and told me about it, but I wasn't hardly listening, and soon enough I couldn't recall a word he'd said or why this was such a cause to celebrate.

A week or two later it was forgotten, and he was onto some other scheme.

So the day the Barrows had come, I knew there was some plan in the works. And it made me frightful uneasy. Pa fooling with backward letters or shiny stones was one thing. But drawing in other folks, especially folks as peculiar as Leon and Noel Barrow, did not bode well.

☾Chapter 6 ✩

THAT NIGHT I WALKED DOWN THE LITTLE WINDING trace behind our cabin. At first I didn't know where I was going. But like other times when I was sore disturbed, I found that going down to the river was a comfort.

Our land backed directly on the Genesee. However, I had to trek a far piece, through our paltry little hayfield and along a flinty creek bed, to reach the banks.

Across the river was just scrubland. I think somebody had farmed those acres for a while, but Pa said they took off west for better land before we arrived. Willows hung their drooping branches down into the water there. The banks were sandy, scoured away every spring by the flooding, so the shape changed year to year.

In summertime I would see arks floating downriver. They'd make up these flat-bottomed boats farther upstream and float barrels of flour or potash all the way to the falls at Rochester, where the goods would be shipped east on the Grand canal. Pa said the arks then got knocked apart and sold for lumber. During the fall the Genesee would coast lazily along, all spangled with red and gold leaves. In winter the river glinted with shards of uptwisted ice. And at night I could hear it creaking as the clear, frozen blades worked against each other.

But it was springtime when I liked the river the best. It's true, sometimes it overspilled the banks and swept away house and barn and destroyed the planted fields. But that's what made our land so fertile, that once-in-a-while flood of rich black river muck. This year there wasn't much threat of a flood. The snows had melted steady, and tho the river was thick and swollen and brown as molasses, unless there were some heavy rains, it would stay within its banks.

So there I stood that night, looking at the river and wondering what would become of me and Pa.

The moon was riding low in the sky. And her twin was riding in the black water too. I thought of Pa's looking glass and how he said everything had a double, a reflection, a backward or forward twin.

It was powerful quiet that night, some would say as still as the tomb. But I didn't fancy that stillness was such a thing to fear. For me it was not deathly like the grave, but alive. Like a baby sleeping in her mother's belly, or the rod of iron waiting to be pounded by the smith, or a keg of gunpowder that will soon make a tremendous noise and fire. It was still like a girl with her eyes closed and not moving, but her head all filled with a thousand thoughts.

At night especially I felt that aching sense of being far away. But far away from what? I don't mean that it took us all day to walk into town and back. Tho of course that added to the aloneness. And I don't mean that I was far away from the other folks because they feared me and whispered and stared when they thought I didn't notice.

At night it seemed we lived in a place where no other people had ever been. I looked up at the moon and thought that somehow I'd been switched. What I mean is, that night I fancied I was on the moon looking at the earth. I know that makes little sense. They say the moon is big and massy like our world. I read that it's cold hard stone with not a speck of life on it. Still, that night in my tangled-up thinking, I wondered, what if I were looking at the earth and really standing on the moon?

I fancied I was the girl on the moon, so many distant leagues away across the inky black sky from the world with all its people and bustle and noise and suchlike.

Perhaps I was dwelling on my pa's notion of twins too much. Mayhap I'd let my mind wander too far, thinking of another Hannah up there on the moon where nobody could see her or even knew she was alive.

I read in one of Pa's books that the moon is a she. The ancient heathen people made her a goddess, not a god. And

I thought how every one of the honeybee workers is a she. And of course the queen is too. I don't know what most folks thought, but I fancied the river was like a mother. She was patient, gentle, and quiet most of the time. Tho once in a long while she could rage fierce and fearless.

I sat by the riverbank, and it seemed that I was alone there in a place that never needed any menfolk nor their labors.

I took care of the fields and our spraddle-legged cow. I cut the firewood for the cooking most of the time. I was the one who climbed on the roof of our shanty in a rainstorm to plug up the holes with moss and scraps of pinewood. I spun the thread and sewed the clothes, tho I must admit I didn't take much pleasure in that.

So, I thought that night, looking at the moon, what need was there for menfolk? My pa had learning, and he taught me to read and reckon with numbers. But I knew that there were times when they had a young woman teach at the school in Little Sion. So that wasn't something we had to have menfolk for.

I'd heard it said that menfolk are needed for hunting, for war and fighting, for preaching the gospel, and for ruling the nation. But where I lived my life, these things seemed most times pretty well useless. Since the war with England, and that was before my time, we had no need of soldiers with their marching and drumming and sticking out their chests like roosters. And in our part of the country, hunting didn't provide hardly any food for the table. We needed to plow and sow and reap, not wander the woods hoping to see a deer we might kill. It's true that preachers are menfolk. But if I understand the Bible stories correctly, there were ladies in the olden days who preached the word. Indeed, wasn't it Mary Magdalene who our Lord appeared to first after he came out from the grave? And as for the governor and president and senators, they were as far away from where I lived as the king of France or the emperor of China. I'd certainly never see any of them, nor would anybody in Black Stick. So did it matter who they were or if they even were made-up stories?

My mind was sore unsettled that night, with thoughts like these. I had a broad flat rock I liked to sit upon. And there I tarried a long while, trying to sort out my confusion.

My pa was a good man. I never once thought otherwise. But still, he was a man. And how could he understand what kind of thoughts a girl would have?

He was going to get himself, and me, into trouble. I knew that as sure as I knew I was sitting there. And I wondered for about the hundredth time: what if my ma were still there? Wouldn't things be better? Wouldn't she hold a tight rein on Pa and keep him from bringing us mischief and affliction? Wouldn't it give me someone to talk to when I felt I was the only one in the whole world?

Chapter 7

ABOUT A WEEK LATER PA LOADED THE WAGON WITH charcoal and went into town. Tho I had nothing to barter with, still I said I wanted to go along with him.

As we rattled and jounced along the track, I breathed deep the scents of the March morning. The sun had melted off the last of the snow patches. Not even in the shade of the dense pines did the little icy crusts remain.

Mim, who did double duty before the plow and the coal wagon, seemed in a tolerable mood that day. Even she could feel the life of the earth coming back. Even a worn-out old horse could sense the ground and the trees and the flowers being born again after their long winter sleep.

Pa, however, didn't share our cheery mood. He usually looked forward to spending the day in Black Stick. He'd haggle with Mr. Harmon and curse the price he got. But afterward he always told me he got the best of the bargain.

Of course he'd inquire if any packages had come for him. If a book had arrived, he was filled with good humor. And if not, he'd have Mr. Harmon fill his jug with whiskey and dwell on this other, lesser, pleasure.

This day, so bright and balmy, he was in a dark and secret, turned-inside humor. I remarked on Seeboom's Branch when we crossed over. Mim splashed through with no complaint. And the sight of the silvery creek, swollen still with spring runoff, did my heart good. But Pa barely noticed and said nothing when I mentioned how pretty it was that morning.

As we drew nearer to Black Stick, his mood grew grimmer. I tried to pretend I didn't see. I even broke into a little song. But this was like the whistling of boys who're walking through a dim and unknown part of the forest. It's a happy sound, but it quakes a little, their fear coloring the music itself.

Pa grunted and growled, and I ceased my singing. We went around the bend and saw Minor's place, which is the last farm before coming into the town proper. Jeremy Minor was out in the near field, walking behind his ox and struggling to keep the plowshare down in the earth. He waved and I waved back, but Pa only murmured about Mr. Minor owing him a half-dollar since two years past.

Still, I clung to my glad state of mind as long as I could. The sight of the wet brown curls of soil turned up by the plow was a happy one. Even the starlings flocking down to feed on the unearthed worms were pleasing to my eyes.

Then we went down the steep incline, Pa pulling hard on the brake lever, and we were in Black Stick.

For a girl who'd been no farther than Little Sion, and that only twice in my life, Black Stick always seemed full of bustle and commerce. I suppose to someone who'd been to a real city, like Albany or Rochester, or to the great metropolis of Manhattan, Black Stick would have seemed a hopeless backwater. But to a girl who spent almost all her days on the farm, and of those, half the time not even seeing her own pa, the village was a most welcome sight.

We went direct to Mr. Harmon's store. First thing Pa asked was if any express packages had come in. To my surprise, there was one with Pa's name written on it. But it was smaller than a book and, by the way he hefted it, lighter too.

Not wanting me to see what was in the package, he told me to make myself scarce.

So I wandered the store and admired all the items that money could buy. In particular, I dwelt on the various dyes that might turn drab homespun cloth into something gladsome to the eye: indigo, saffron, madder root, and various powders I had never heard of.

Pa and Mr. Harmon went outside and circled round the wagon, dickering over the price of charcoal. Their voices rose and fell, and I heard a note of anxiousness in Pa's that I'd never heard before.

But then Phoebe Cale came into the store, and we set to talking. I asked her about her dog Hercules, who had been pretty well mauled a few months back. "Poppa says it was a wolf that Herky got into a scrap with. He's still limping a bit, poor thing." The wolves had been pretty well run out of our part of York State. Once in a while, however, we'd hear that somebody's sheep was dragged off.

Phoebe was usually kind to me if her mother wasn't around. Or if the other young folks in the village didn't see her with me. There, in the cool darkness of Mr. Harmon's store, she was friendly and didn't show any sign she had to go off. Indeed, she took me into a corner to tell me the big news about Melissa Crane.

"She's gone," Phoebe whispered. "She went off with the school master, Mr. Samuels. I couldn't hardly believe such a thing. She's only a year older than me, and she fled last month with Mr. Samuels. Her poppa got all the men together and guns and horses to chase them down, but last I heard they still haven't been found. He must be twice her age. And such a gawky man, stiff as a ramrod. Why would she do such a thing?"

I wasn't surprised that Phoebe cared more about Mr. Samuels's appearance than about his character.

"He's not the most comely man I've ever seen," I said. "That's for certain. But he's traveled around the country, I heard. He lived in Boston for a while, didn't he? And New York City, and Baltimore too. I fancy that Melissa wanted to see the rest of the world. If she married a boy from Black

Stick or Little Sion, she'd never get more than a dozen miles from the place she was born."

"But it's such a scandal!" Phoebe said. "To run off like that. Her father calls her a harlot and says if she ever comes back, he won't let her over his doorstep."

Just then, Mrs. Cale walked into the store and called for Phoebe. We came out from the corner, and Mrs. Cale gave us a grim look.

"I was just passing the time with Hannah," Phoebe said.

"I can see that," her mother said. She was not happy that I would speak with Phoebe, but she tried to be polite. "You need to be home this instant, Phoebe. There's chores enough waiting to last you a week. Now you get along."

Phoebe obeyed, scurrying past without even saying goodbye.

Mrs. Cale regarded me with a foul look, as tho I'd sought her daughter out to pour evil in her ear. "You're just in town for a little while?" she asked.

I nodded.

"That's good," she said. "I'm sure you're happier back at home." And with that she left.

Chapter 8

PA WAS DONE UNLOADING THE CHARCOAL BY THEN.
He had his little package, and he'd filled his jug with spirits.
But he didn't seem ready to go back home.

He said, "Ah, there you are, daughter. Come along." He
left Mim and the wagon and led me down the road. Across
from the meetinghouse was a tavern where Pa sometimes
went to drink. This was a hovel of a place, not much better
than a den for wild beasts. The few times I'd been in town
at night, I'd heard loud cries and shouts from the tavern,
men fighting and women screeching. When Pa went there,
I stayed outside. My curiosity did eat at me, but I knew it
would only make me more distressed to see my pa in such
dire circumstances.

Next door was a cooperage. Martin McNair worked there,
fashioning barrels to ship our flour north, kegs for whiskey,
and fine, smooth butter tubs. Mr. McNair was a quiet man,
tall and thin as a broom. With the wheat growing so well, he

always had work. And day or night you could hear the rasp of his hatchet as he smoothed barrel staves or the thud of his hammer as he worked them tight together.

Pa led me in that direction, not saying a word. But soon enough I saw why we were going there. Out from Mr. McNair's shop came the two Barrow brothers.

There in town, they didn't seem so much like twin ogres as they had at our cabin. I believe they'd both shaved that morning and slicked their hair back. They'd cleaned the dust and field dirt off their boots too.

Noel, the older one, greeted Pa. Leon hung back a little. He didn't do much talking that day, letting his big brother speak for both of them.

"You didn't tell no lies, Ace." That's how the menfolk at the tavern said my pa's name, which was really Asa. "She's a fair-looking girl. And she's no weeping willow. She's like an oak that won't bend, if what we seen the other week is a true sign."

"But she's got sweetness too," Pa said. I'd never in all my life heard him say that. Sweetness? I thought, what did he know about such things?

"Since Mrs. Renner's been gone," Pa went on, "Hannah has been a steady blessing to me. She's not much for spinning and sewing, but she can make fine, sweet apple fritters."

Listening to this, I almost thought Pa was drunk. He didn't ever talk this way about me. He didn't curse and complain much, but I'd never heard such good things.

So far, neither of the Barrows had even said their greeting

to me. They were talking about me as if I was stony-deaf or worse, something that couldn't think or understand, like the farmyard beasts.

"I want to go home now, Pa," I said.

He ignored this, talking more to the Barrows, saying all kinds of good things about me.

"I'm going now," I said. "I'll take Mim and the wagon and you can walk."

I turned to get away from them, but Pa took ahold of me by the shoulder. "You stay where you stand, daughter." His grip was tight, and it got tighter as I pulled. "We'll go back home when I say so."

"I don't want to be here no more." Then I looked at the Barrow brothers. Noel grinned at me like menfolk do when they watch a feisty little dog sicced on a bear for sport. I suppose he was enjoying the sight of Pa and me going at it.

"She's a fierce one too," Noel said. "Might have a sweet voice, but she'll bite like a rattler when you get her riled." At this, his brother laughed. It sounded like somebody pounding on an empty barrel.

"Mayhap you better get along, Ace. Don't want her all bereft with anger."

Pa scowled at this. "She'll obey. She'll do what she's told. She knows about a daughter's duty to her father."

"Still, we don't want her all riled," Noel said, grinning.

"Here," Noel said. "We brought you something." He held out a book. "Go on and take it. We got no use for it."

"What my brother is trying to say is it's a present."

I thought perhaps I had a fever and was not seeing and hearing quite right. Pa seemed so strange. And the brothers, who I hardly knew, were giving me a gift when it wasn't Christmas nor the anniversary of my birthday. I didn't care if I never saw them again, and there they were giving me a gift.

"Take it, daughter. It's not right to refuse a present."

"I don't want nothing from them," I said real quiet.

"Your pa said you like to read, and he said you got a pleasing tone for singing." Noel held the book out to me.

"Go on," Leon said. "We got no use for it."

"Because you can't read?" I asked. "And got voices like bullfrogs?"

"Take it!" Pa growled. "You do as you're told." He hardly ever used that kind of voice on me. But when he did, I knew better than to say no.

I stepped forward and accepted the book. It was called *Wyeth's Repository of Music*.

"Now can we go home, Pa? Please? I don't want to be here no more."

He told me to say thank you, which I did, probably too quiet for the brothers to hear. And then he headed back toward the wagon. I followed a few steps behind. I surely had no use for presents from the Barrows. But I hung on to the book, and as we rattled back home on the wagon, I paged through and even sang a song or two under my breath.

Chapter 9

AS SOON AS WE GOT HOME, PA TOOK THE LITTLE package he'd got express and disappeared into the woods. He didn't come home for dinner that night, and I didn't see him at all the next day.

I did my work. But a few times I washed my hands off at the well, went back to the cabin, and looked through the book the Barrows had given me.

I had a songster that sometimes I liked to sing from. But it had no music, just words. This book by Mr. Wyeth had notes too and an explanation about the different shapes and what they meant. I found one song I already knew by heart, "Old Hundredth," and by singing it and comparing the shapes with other songs, I learned "Wondrous Love," "Mear," and "New Jordan."

This made my heart a little gladder. But the whole time, I was trying not to think about my pa and why he'd acted so strange, nor the Barrows and why they would give me this book.

I went out to the fire yard that night and saw no sign that Pa had been working there. A wind had come up, and it blew the cold ashes this way and that like a snowstorm. I could hardly see the moon through the swirling white clouds. There's a place talked about in the Bible called Gehenna. It's where refuse and trash was burnt outside the city. But it was also another name for the Devil's realm. I stood there looking at the little cyclones of ash and dust, listening to the weird sky howls, and thought of my pa spending all his time there in the Gehenna he made with his own hands.

It was the next day that he came home.

And he looked like he really had been to the infernal place. His clothes were more soiled than usual, his face was washed out pale like somebody who had the consumption. He staggered into the cabin and slumped down by the fire. At first I just thought he'd been on another drunk. But then I didn't smell any spirits on him, nor did he moan and shake like he did when he'd had too much to drink.

I asked him where he'd been, but he didn't answer.

"Pa, I'm talking to you. Where you been to?"

He shook his head, not like he wouldn't talk but like he didn't even know how. Then I saw a little silver shine in the palm of his hand. I came closer and asked him what it was. He showed me: a big coin, but not like any money I'd ever seen.

I thought, of course, that he'd finally found what he'd

been searching for. Money, silver, and gold were what he wanted. And here was the proof, or so I thought, that his searching was not foolishness.

But he didn't seem the least bit gladdened by the coin.

I asked where he'd found it and he said, "Didn't find it. I bought it."

"From who'd you buy such a thing? This makes no sense, Pa. Why would you buy money?"

"It's not money. It's an amulet." He showed me, holding it in the light of the fire. All around the edge were strange little letters that he told me were in the Hebrew language. And in the middle was a serpent wound around a stick. "It's not money. I bought it to help find treasure. If I can reckon out the mystery, then I'll never have to cut another log or burn another rick. And you won't have to plow or cook or wash our clothes. We'll be rich, Hannah, richer than you can imagine."

"You spent our money on that?" Sheer foolishness, that's what it was. The folly of a man bereft of all sense. "We hardly got seed corn for next year and I don't have decent shoes to wear for Sunday meeting, and you waste our money on such a thing?"

He knew I'd lash him with my tongue. He expected that my vexation would know no bounds.

"It'll find us treasure, Hannah. That's what the man said in his letter. Treasure such as you never seen."

"If it works so well, then why would he sell it?"

"Because he didn't know the proper uses. He didn't study the books like I have."

Of course I asked him where all this treasure was. And of course he didn't have any.

"Pa, where did you get the money for that? Not from selling charcoal."

And when he told me, my wrath rose up like a thunderhead. "You sold off part of our land to buy this foolishness?" Seven acres of fine woods and a few already cut down and ready for the plow. "You threw away our land for this?"

He didn't fight back, for he knew he'd made a terrible mistake. The day before he must have wandered the woods and fields with this amulet, chanting his secret words and waving his hands. And of course he hadn't found a thing. He'd got more and more desperate, thinking of what he'd done and what I'd say, but finally he knew he had to come home.

"You sold off all that woodland you could turn into a mountain of charcoal for that foolish little bit of metal? I imagine it's not even silver, but cheap pewter. Give it here." I held it up to the light. I didn't know much about coins and money, but it looked like a little bauble they might use to trick Indians into selling their birthright.

Then I asked him who he'd sold the land to.

He didn't say at first, so it was easy to guess. "The Barrows? You sold our good land to those two? Oh, Pa, how could you do something so foolish?" And my wrath melted into tears, and I knelt there on the rough, splintery boards of the floor and wept. I held on to him by the knees, and I wept for myself and for him and for the beautiful woods I'd never have anymore.

☾ Chapter 10

PA DISAPPEARED AGAIN THE NEXT DAY. I WENT TO the fire yards, but he wasn't there. I wandered the wooded acres he'd given away, but he wasn't to be found there either. I went down to the river and called for him. I even walked a ways along the path to Black Stick. Still, there was no sign of him.

He wasn't a bad man, I kept telling myself. He meant well. But he was like a child sometimes. And I was the mother, taking care of him. He didn't want me to spend my life drudging in the fields and living in a leaky old shanty. He wanted a fine house and servants to do my chores. But the only way he knew to get such a thing was to hunt up and down for some treasure that nobody really believed was real.

I slept poorly that night, all alone in the shanty. I had a dream about my ma, tho it was all blown away like smoke in a strong breeze when I awoke. I didn't have any recollection of her face. But there was a lady in my dream who I knew was my ma.

That morning it was powerful cold. I had to break a thin scum of ice on the pitcher to wash my face. And my hands were clumsy and numb when I tried to make a fire.

I mixed up cornmeal and salt and a little bit of lard, and I poured boiling water over it to make johnnycake dough. Then when the coals were bright and crimson-orange, I formed the little cakes and baked them.

After these were done and cooling off, I took care of the beasts and split up some wood for the fire. But the whole time that morning, I felt something was dire wrong. It was Pa, of course. He'd looked terrible dejected when I scolded him so severe for buying that foolish amulet. He seemed ashamed for wasting his money. Worse, for giving up the land I'd have to live on when I was grown-up.

The whole time I worked that morning, it gnawed away at me like a dog gnaws at a bone. Where was he, I kept asking myself. What was going to happen?

Then I came back into the cabin. I saw the book the Barrows had given to me. And it was plain to me like the sun is plain in the noonday sky. He was over to the Barrows' place. I knew this all along, I suppose. But I didn't want to admit it. I didn't want to think of him over there making another foolish bargain.

I wrapped up the johnnycakes in a rag, put on my shoes,

and grabbed that book. I was out the door before I knew where I was going. I was heading to the Barrows' place, of course. I'd set my mind on straightening this all out. I'd give that book back to them, tho I did surely enjoy the songs inside. And I'd give Pa an earful, demanding he come home.

The walk to the Barrows' was long. It was in the opposite direction from Black Stick, and so I didn't see a single soul along the way. Some of the land had been cut or burnt. But much of the way, I walked along a forest trace hardly wide enough for a horse to pass by. Robins were singing and willows brightening with green buds. But I hardly noticed the spring's awakening, being so set on straightening Pa and the Barrows out.

I had to cross Gat's Creek over a fallen log. And for a little space of time, I stood there poised on the quaking little bridge. Up one way was an abandoned mill. The wheel hung broken, furred over with glistening moss.

Turning carefully, I looked in the other direction and saw a kind of rainbow above the creek. The water splashed over rocks, and the sun was at just the right angle to make a beautiful arc of colors there.

In the Bible it says the rainbow was God's sign of favor. So I took this to mean that my mission would turn out for the best.

In about an hour I had reached the Barrows' place. It was down in a wild, lost sort of dell. Grapevines tangled over the pathway, making a kind of tunnel. Then I was out in the sunlight again, but it had a different quality, it seemed, thinner and weaker, kind of watery.

The Barrows' house was much bigger than ours, with a high pitched roof all grown over with moss. As I came closer, the house seemed to shine. It was a black-purple kind of shimmer, like the feathers of a grackle standing in sunlight. They had two glass windows in the front, round like portholes on a ship.

I slowed down seeing the house. I wasn't so sure anymore. Could I grab Pa by the ear as if he was a mischievous boy and drag him home? Could I fling down that book and say to the Barrows, "I don't want any presents from the likes of you"?

I considered for a minute that I should just turn around and forget my mission that day. Was I getting as foolish as Pa coming all the way there?

Then Noel came out from the doorway and spied me at the wood's edge. He called to his brother, and Leon too appeared.

"You come to sing us one of those songs from the book?" he asked.

I was silent. What was I doing there? I thought. Had my Pa's softheaded ways started to rub off on me?

"That's right," Noel said, noticing I had the book with me. "She come to give us a little concert."

I straightened up and said in a loud, steady voice, "Is my pa here? He's got to come home."

They smiled at that. Noel ducked his head in the house, and I heard him shouting, "Ace, hey Ace, your little girl is here looking for you."

Then Pa came out too. He looked washed out and kind of bent over, as if he'd aged ten years in a week. He signaled for me to come near.

"I wasn't going to fetch you till tomorrow. But this way is fine," he said.

"What are you talking about?" I asked. "You come home now, and I'll fix you some food. And you get some sleep, and things'll be just fine." But neither of us believed my words.

"No." He took hold of me by the hand and said, "You come in here."

The Barrows nodded their agreement. "We was just talking about you," Noel said.

"Pa, come on home now." A little while before, I was all set to fix things straight. I'd been so sure and steady. Now all that seemed utter folly. I should have stayed home, I said to myself. I should have let Pa do as he pleased and stayed out of his affairs.

The three men stood together, looking intent at me. It was strange, but I felt like I was peering into three different looking glasses. From the expression on Noel's face, you'd have thought I was the prize lamb and he the hungry wolf.

Pa's look wasn't craving like that. He saw me as something valuable, but something he could hold or dispose of as he pleased. Leon's face was harder to read. To him, I guessed, I was a threat, something good but maybe a little dangerous.

"Come on inside," Noel said. And Pa led me into their house.

The main room was twice the height of ours. A fire was guttering, and one candle flickered on a wall sconce. The floor was strewn with straw and shavings. Through the two round windows a little light streamed. Something was rattling around in the shadows. But I didn't think it was a dog or a cat.

Again I told Pa he had to come home. Again the brothers grinned and Pa shook his head. "Sit down, daughter," he said. When he called me that, I knew there was nothing I could do to change his mind. He looked sickly and pale, but there was an iron hardness about him that day which scared me severe.

"It's good you came all by yourself. I didn't fancy having to tote you here."

"What are you talking about, Pa?" I was near to weeping already before he even said the words I was dreading to hear.

"You know I been studying on treasures and lost gold for a long while. And Leon and Noel been real interested in the work too."

The brothers stood behind Pa, huge and broad in the quaking light. They nodded as Pa spoke.

46

"It's a good thing you came today. It's a good sign that this will work out for the best."

"Pa, let's go home." My hands were shaking.

"This is your home now, daughter."

"What are you talking about?"

"This is where you live now. It's all arranged. From now on this is your home."

Chapter 11

HE SAID IT SIMPLE AND PLAIN AND STRAIGHT. BUT he might as well have told me I was to be locked away in the deepest dungeon. Again I said we should go home. And again Pa said that the Barrows' place was my new home.

"But why do we got to live here, Pa? Did you sell off all our land?"

Leon laughed kind of uneasy, and his brother shushed him.

Pa said that he hadn't sold any more land. "Then why we got to leave our home?"

"I'm going back home, Hannah," he said quiet as smoke rising up a chimney. "I won't be that far away. You can come to visit at home sometimes."

Then the tears came. Alone in this house with the Barrow brothers? Of course I asked him why. But his answer didn't make any sense. I was to work there as a servant girl, cooking and cleaning and spinning and tending to the beasts.

"We made an arrangement," he said. My tears ran like liquid fire down my face. How could he sell me off this way like a sheep or a pig?

I told him if he wanted money, I'd work harder at home at the spinning wheel and we could sell my wares. "Why, Pa, why?" I kept gasping at him.

"It's not forever, Hannah. Just a year. That's the arrangement we made. A year here, and then we'll have everything we ever wanted."

So it was another of his treasure-hunting schemes. He'd sold me off for another amulet or secret map or book full of foolishness. The tears didn't let up, but now it was wrath and grief all mixed up together in me. I yelled at him and then broke down in sniveling. I begged him and cursed him. I asked him why, and I told him I wouldn't do it. I'm sure I was a sight to behold, by turns raging and weeping.

In the end, tho, there was nothing I could do to break his will. He didn't threaten or call me daughter, as he did when he was angry. I could see there was real sadness in him for what he'd done. But there was no turning back now. "The deal is struck," he said. "Only one year, and then you can come home."

I looked around the Barrows' house. A whole year in this place would be an eternity. Yes, it was bigger than our cabin, and I imagined they had more food and by the look of the hearth, better furnishings. But it wasn't home, and it would be with these two great hulking men who I hardly even knew. A servant girl? Scrubbing and grubbing all day?

Tears and curses came again, for my pa and for the Barrows. But this was feeble, like a puppy dog yapping at a bear.

"They've got a room all ready for you," Pa said. "In the back of the house."

One last time I asked why.

"I told you already," Pa said. "It's only a year. And then you can come home and you'll see, we'll have everything we ever wanted."

Chapter 12

HE LEFT ME ALL ALONE THERE AFTER SAYING HE'D BE BACK
in a day or two with my other dress and a few of my books
and favorite things.

And with the closing of the door, the room became still as
a painting. The brothers appeared awkward, not sure what
to do with me. Maybe they were thinking they should set
me to work that instant to get all they could out of me. Or
maybe they considered on making me feel more at home.
Or they might even have been thinking they'd made a terrible mistake taking such a girl into their house.

But they just stood there like two statues.

I sniffed back my tears and wiped my eyes on my sleeve.
I took a deep breath, like I did before setting to work on
some hard and obnoxious chore. Then I said, "So where am
I to stay?"

My voice broke them out of their trance. And they both

spoke at the same time. Not understanding either of them, I asked again. After getting a foul look from his older brother, Leon stayed mum.

Noel said, "There's a room around back. The chimney runs through one wall, so it stays tolerable warm in the winter. And you have a window."

I told them to show me. Noel led the way.

The room could have been much worse. There was a bed and a little stand for the washbasin. This was made of better pottery than anything we had at home. Like the rest of the house, the walls were raw planks, but they'd been cut and fitted with some skill, so there weren't many cracks that needed chinking up with clay.

And indeed there was a window, made of real glass. It was round, like the two in the main room, and looked out on the back lands. It was wilder here, far from Black Stick. Much of the woods was still uncut. And past the near meadow was a stand of huge old birch trees. Their bark was pure white, and in the afternoon sun they seemed to glow with a beautiful light.

I told the brothers that I'd set to making dinner shortly. "Now you get out of my room," I said.

There I was, bereft of everything I loved. But I was determined I'd have something of my own. "I'll do my chores here like my pa said. I'm a hard worker. But I want you two to promise me you'll never ever come into this room as long as I stay here."

Noel was about to speak, but I told him to be quiet. "Never. Do you understand me? I'll fetch your water and weave your cloth and grind your grain. But you can never ever come into this room."

After my tears, they were surprised by this standing up for myself. "I don't know what your arrangement is with Pa. But we need to have one too. Right now, both of you swear you won't never come in this room."

I suppose one of them, with just one hand, could have picked me up and shook me like a little corn husk doll. But that day there were no threats, no demands, no puffing out their chests and bellowing like bulls.

"Swear!" I said.

And they did.

Chapter 13

THE ROOM HAD A PROPER DOOR ON IT, NOT LIKE MY sleeping loft at home with just a raggedy old curtain. Shutting the door, I wondered how I might fashion a latch to give myself a bit more privacy.

When I sat down on the bed, I had a straight view out the little round window. The glass had streaks in it. The soft twists and blebs in the windowpane gave the back lands a gentle, misty look. I liked what I saw: a field where the Barrows' ox stood, still as the boulders beyond, and at the far reaches, the stand of beautiful white-boled birches.

I got up and pressed my face to the window. My breath fogged the view even more, and it might have been a rainy dusktime out there.

Then I heard voices, Noel and Leon arguing. I heard the word *wench*, and I supposed that meant me. I heard shouts and words that I supposed must be curses, by their loudness and fierceness. I heard Noel tell his brother he must submit, because Leon was the younger one. And then there was a long silence.

I stared out the window until I saw the brothers go to the fields to work. Then I went to the hearth and started in to make them some dinner.

Chapter 14

I ASKED THEM WHAT THE DATE WAS SO THAT WE might fix my term of service exactly. Neither one of them could read, tho, so studying the almanack would be useless.

"There's three hundred and sixty-five days to the year," I said. "I'm going to take a piece of smooth pinewood and cut a notch for every day I work here. And when the last notch is carved, I'll leave." So there was most of the springtime, then summer and fall and the long winter before I could return home. "One year," I said. "And not one day more."

They agreed to this with solemn nods and set back to work eating their pork and corn bread. I'd found a smatter of young leeks and adder tongues growing in the wet flats near the river. These I added to their dinner, probably the first greens they'd had since the autumn time.

They gulped the food down like dogs afraid somebody will yank their bones away. They drank cider, but being such great huge men, not enough to get them drunk. When the meal was over, their faces were covered with grease and crumbs. Leon grabbed for the last crust of corn bread, and his brother smashed his hand hard and snatched it up for himself.

"I'll make more next time," I said and cleared away the bowls and cups. Leon stared at his brother with eyes full of hate. Then he grabbed the black iron kettle and stuck his hand in to scrape up the last of the pot liquor. His brother cuffed him in the back of the head. As he shouted "Mind your manners!" crumbs and spittle blew out of his mouth.

They were still growling and cursing each other when I went outside to the well to fetch water for the cleaning up.

Chapter 15

I LAY IN MY BED THAT NIGHT THINKING AND THINKING. Of course I wanted to know why I was sent off like a slave sold to some new master. I told myself it was just one of Pa's crazy schemes, and when I got home I'd make sure there were never any more. I'd reckon out a way to keep him under my eye.

But I couldn't help thinking there was something wrong with me to deserve this fate. Like with my strange eyes, it seemed I was guilty of something I didn't even know about. The old women in Black Stick muttered about the sins of the father meted out to the new generation, as if it was some plague passed along from parents to children. But Pa wasn't a bad man, just foolish sometimes. He'd never done anything to bring down a curse on us.

Then I thought maybe it was my ma. I hardly knew a thing about her. Pa never liked to talk of her much. It got him somber with black grief. Perhaps there was a curse on her that I was now suffering under.

All I knew about her could be said in a minute or two. She'd come out to York State with my pa right after they got married. It was early on, when there still were Seneca living here and there, tho the fighting was over by then. They'd set up a farmstead and had their first baby, my sister, Nan, who I don't remember at all. My ma had her heart full of religion. Or so I gathered from all the Bible books and flimsy little paper tracts that she left behind. She grew up in the good righteous Methodist Church, but strange kinds of religion were brewing in the west of York State. I heard about a beautiful lady who called herself the Universal Friend and had a whole colony of followers, as if she was the queen and they the workers and drones. And there was the traveling preacher Lorenzo Dow, who stayed at our place one time and gave me a blessing and said he'd pass by our way some other day. There were strange prophets like the one called Mathias, who they said killed a man in New York City and fled west.

And then there was Joe Smith and his Golden Bible, which he found over at Palmyra. When I was still too little to remember, he stirred up a whole flock of believers. He preached his message, and soon there were dozens of them hereabouts. Some sold their farms to pay for publishing the new Bible. Some went from town to town talking about their new kind of faith. And some gave up their families and went off with him to his new promised land.

To Pa's and my eternal sadness, my ma was one of those who had heard and believed the new message. She gave us up and went off, and I heard folks say that Joe Smith had ten or twenty wives in his brand-new holy city. And if Pa's drunken weeping had any truth to it, she forswore her marriage to him and became one of Joe Smith's new wives.

Pa talked about this only twice or thrice that I remember. He was "hard under the bootheel," as he called it those times. Others said more plainly he was drunk. It was true that the whiskey made him talk and sometimes cry like a little child. He wept for me, who had no ma. He wept for his lonesome self. He wept for Ma and Nan, gone off with Joe Smith to some promised land in the far-west wilderness. And so I'd have to comfort him, saying "There, there, don't cry" to a grown man who should have been comforting me.

Why, I often wondered, did Ma take Nan and not me when she went off with the westward-going saints? Of course, folks in Black Stick gossiped about such a scandalous happening, but mostly it was lies. Why, I often lay awake wondering, did I get left behind and not taken to the promised land? Would the new saints there have nothing to do with a queer-eyed girl? Was there something bad in me? Did I deserve to be left behind?

I knew the story of Passover from the Bible, how the angel

of death went from house to house, killing or saving depending on the mark on the door. So, I wondered, was the prophet like that angel, choosing who would suffer and who would enjoy happiness? But it got confusing, because I'd wonder if I was passed over from being slain or from being saved.

At home, I slept in the overloft with a curtain hanging to make it a room of my own. But I could hear Pa snoring loud as a bucksaw in wet pinewood. You could fire a rifle three inches from his ear, and still he wouldn't wake up. So he never once heard me crying up in my loft, crying to think of Ma in some golden holy city out west, the beautiful bride of the prophet, and me there in the dirty, drafty cabin.

I thought, of course, I'd been passed over on account of my eyes. But once in a while, even with all my heartache, I told myself they weren't a curse but a sign of favor. I couldn't then have explained it in words, but being different that way was actually a blessing.

These, and a hundred other thoughts, churned around in my head while I lay in my new bed.

A strange kind of light shone into the room through my little window. The moon was up that night, a pale little sickle sharp at both ends. I cupped my hands lying there and held the moonlight as if it was water. And I fell asleep that way, washed in the whiteness.

Chapter 16

THE NEXT DAY WORK WAS PRETTY MUCH ENDLESS. After I made the brothers a breakfast of corn mush and bacon grease, I had to boil water for washing and to get bread rising for their dinner.

When that was done, I went out and saw the brothers hauling beech logs from the wood lot. One on each side of the great moaning saw, they cut the logs into two-foot lengths. Then it was my task to split these for firewood. I was a fair hand with the ax, and back at home I could manage a small splitting maul. But the brothers were twice my pa's size, and I couldn't even budge their maul. So I cleaved some small cracks in the logs, placed in the wedges, and pounded with a mallet.

When I had enough wood for the day, Noel growled at me to follow him to one of the outbuildings. There, in the dim light, was one of their pigs, dead and hanging from a chain attached to a rafter.

Underneath was a bucket, collecting blood. Leon was cutting the brute into slabs with a saw. The roof was too low for him. And joined by his brother, he was crowded in close to the pig. Both were soon crimson to the arms, grunting and huffing as they cut. The scene was terrible to behold: two huge men seeming to let loose all their stored-up wrath on the poor carcass of the beast.

I'd helped Pa salt and smoke our meat. But our beasts were much smaller, and the slaughtering didn't seem so awful a thing.

Noel nodded to a slab of meat lying on a wood plank. "That's for salting. I'll take care of the smoking."

So I grabbed the meat in both hands and lugged it up to the house. There, I filled a barrel with water from the well. I wasn't sure how much salt to put in. My pa had said it had to be briny enough to float an egg. But the Barrows didn't have chickens. So I had to guess at it. I looked around the kitchen for molasses and, finding a little crock, added some to the pickling water. I knew the meat had to stay under the whole time, so I found a smooth rock by the well, washed it off as best I could, and rested it on the meat to keep it under.

I went back to get another slab. This went on all afternoon, trudging back and forth, pushing the meat down in the brine-water, until I was as filthy and sticky with blood as the brothers.

By the time we were done, I had to get their evening meal cooking. Fresh pork, roasted on a spit over the fire, would have been a treat. But when the brothers were done gorging themselves, there wasn't much left for me. All I got were scraps and grease on the big wooden platter, which I mopped up with biscuits.

Chapter 17

I FELL ASLEEP LIKE A ROCK DROPPED INTO A WELL. I think the brothers were still up, arguing with and cursing each other as they seemed to do at every free moment. But sleep came for me quick and heavy.

When the moon rose, it drew me up from my dreams. The house was silent then. I got up and looked into the big room. The hearth coals were still glowing orange. I banked them up so they'd be ready the next morning. Then I went back to my room, closed my door, and looked out my window.

Tho I'd never seen it, I imagined this was what the ocean looked like, waves of brilliance and darkness.

I stood there awhile, with my blanket wound around me like an Indian gown. Just as I was drifting back to sleep, I saw something moving out by the great birch trees.

At first I thought it was a dog, skulking along from a pool of moonlight to a swath of moon shadow. But looking closer,

I saw it plainly was no dog. A wolf? I wondered. I'd only seen one or two in my whole life, but there were still some in the back lands. Or a panther, I thought. These were as rare as unicorns in York State. A peddler had come through the year before and for a penny would unwrap a bundle he had in his cart. Inside was a panther's head, mouth propped open with sticks to show the fearsome teeth. Pa thought it worth the penny for my education. So I saw what other girls in town had only heard about. It looked like a tomcat, but one you'd see in a nightmare. Three times as big, it was, and with tufts of bristly fur and front teeth as long as my fingers.

I pressed my face to the window, and the shape disappeared. But I waited. And presently it appeared again, closer to the house this time. This was no panther nor wolf. It walked on two legs, tho in a strange, hunched-forward sort of way. At first I thought it was trying to stay hidden as it moved. But then I noticed a pattern to its path. It was going from one patch of light to the other, like a man on a checkerboard.

For a little heartbeat's time he looked directly at me, right at the window. Our eyes locked, or so I thought. And I felt a joyful, liquidy chill in myself. The only thing I could compare it to was the singing at a revival service the Reverend Dow had the last day he was at Black Stick. I was giving my all to the sound, a loud, almost crazy outpouring. All around the camp meeting ground, torches were burning, and the singing seemed to pull me upward. The Reverend Dow had called this the wild ride to Heaven. And that night I thought nothing could be that wonderful.

But there I was in the dark, in the beautiful midnight silence, and I felt something akin to that feeling.

Then the figure was gone.

I told myself it was just a dream, or a freak of the shadow. Living in that place with those brothers had already disordered my mind. There's no wild boys dancing in the midnight shimmers, I told myself. Just go on back to bed. The sun'll be up soon enough, and you've got enough work for two girls tomorrow.

Still, I lingered at the window. I looked out until the moon was swallowed up in a cloud and sleep was rising in me like water filling a well. I went back to bed and had no more dreams that night.

Chapter 18

THE NEXT DAY, AFTER MY USUAL WORK, I HAD TO HELP Noel and Leon finish up with the pig they'd slaughtered. The hams and bacon and big-sized slabs of meat were all smoked or salted. But there remained bones and skin, the head, and the grease to be cooked for lard. And they wanted to make sausages, which was something I'd never seen done.

They set me to washing the pig's guts out, which was certainly a sickening chore. Then they had me take two knives and start to chopping all the pig parts that would get stuffed into the casings. It was endless work, up and down, up and down with the knives, and filthy too. Noel worked at the big iron pot, where he stirred up the red-brown muck. They threw a few handfuls of herbs into the pot, dried-up leaves and pods. They added fresh fat right off the pig, then sent me to hunt up some wild leeks down by the creek bed.

We were at it all afternoon in the back shed while Leon cut more hickory wood to build up a fine thick cloud in the smokehouse.

As I worked, chopping and then stuffing the slippery casings, I'd once in a while take a look beyond the dim, drab shed. It was there, in the open space between the house and the outbuildings, that I'd seen the figure moving the night before. I didn't see any footprints, or even places where the grass was pressed down.

There I was hunched over a great churning pot of chopped-up pig, my hair greasy and my arms stained to the elbows. There were the brothers, working like great heavy machines. They huffed and sucked in air louder than the bellows at a blacksmith's forge. They worked tirelessly, as if driven by a steam engine. There we slaved in the shadowy shed. And now and then I'd look to the place where my nighttime visitor had moved with his secret dreamy grace.

It's strange, but those first few days I never once asked myself, Who is he? The question didn't occur to me. I just dwelt on my memory, seeing him again and again. I didn't wonder, Does he have a name? or Where does he comes from?

Pa once had me read one of his books about the sea and the great ships that travel over the watery globe. And this, what I'd seen at night, put me in mind of a story about a sailor. He'd seen a mermaid, tho the other sailors all said he was just homesick or drunk. But he was sure she'd been real. And like me that day, while the sailor did his work, the memory of the mermaid was more real than any rope or bucket of mop water.

Chapter 19

THAT NIGHT I WOKE ONCE AND PEERED OUT MY
window a long while. But I saw nothing. I banked the coals
and went back to bed. I slept with no dreams and woke to
the sound of the brothers' grumbling and coughing and rattling dishes.

One of them pounded on my door and growled, "Where's
our breakfast?"

I threw on my clothes and got to work fast, all the while
feeling their black and angry eyes on me. Breakfast was not
good, and they told me so. But soon enough they were out
in the fields, and I had the house to myself awhile. I had
much work to do, but at least I could do it without stares
and mutterings.

Later that day my pa showed up on the doorstep. I'd only
been there at the Barrows' a few days, but already something had changed between him and me. Maybe it was just

my wrath at being sold like a slave. Maybe it had taken root and grown and wound around my heart like a thorny vine. I'm not sure. But there was no joy in seeing him. It didn't even occur to me that he was there to take me home. No, my servitude was set for one year, and it would last not one day shorter.

"What do you want?" I said. "Tired already of your own cooking?"

He shook his head. "I came to see how you were getting along."

"What do you expect me to say? 'Everything is just fine'? I work like a slave for two big man-brutes who fight and curse all day. I have not a minute of time to myself. I think about my real home and Mim and once in a while about you too. I want to go home, but you sold me for some worthless trinket."

He stood on the doorstep. I didn't make way for him to come inside. "I got too much work to bandy words with you," I said.

"Hannah," he said like a whipped schoolboy. "Don't talk that way to your pa. Soon enough, real soon, we'll have treasure so great you won't ever—"

I told him to hush. I couldn't listen to that kind of talk. "I got clothes to wash and wood to split, and I'm sure the brothers have a hundred other chores waiting for me."

"Hannah, don't be this way. It's going to be fine. Truly. It'll be fine. You'll see."

"You got any more to say?" He shook his head, and I closed the door. His coming there of course had made me more homesick. If I could just keep my mind on my work, then maybe I could endure this. But with him showing up, talking, and looking for kind words, it was harder to keep my mind clear.

I got the big wash pot boiling and started in on the brothers' filthy clothes. I slapped and beat them on a big rock so hard it sounded like gunshots. I boiled them again and wrung them dry as if wringing the head off a chicken. Tighter and tighter till not a drop of water came out. Then I laid them out on bushes to dry and got on with my other chores.

Chapter 20

THAT NIGHT THE MOON WOKE ME AGAIN, A PALE WASH of light creeping over my face. I got up with the blanket dragging like the train of a robe and peered out my little window.

There he was again. He didn't move graceful like a girl who knows she's pretty and everybody's looking. Not like somebody who's learned to dance the quadrille. There was a grace to him, however, the grace I've seen in forest beasts.

But unlike a skulking badger or wolf, he didn't stay in the shadows. He seemed unafraid, proud even, like he wanted to be seen.

As he came closer to my window, I got a clearer look at his face. He seemed not quite a man but no longer a boy either. His long blond hair was exactly the color of moonlight on snow. And it waved back and forth like a horse's tail.

I pressed my face to the window, and he saw me.

He stopped dead still. And his clothes, which had been fluttering like flags, hung limp off his thin frame. He looked directly at me, and I thought I saw him smile.

Gathering up my blanket, I ran from my room and out the door of the house. But when I came around the corner, there was no one to be seen.

I stood there awhile, listening. Perhaps he'd hidden. But no, there was nothing but long stripes of moonlight.

Back in my room, I gave another look through the window. I thought perhaps that I could see him only through that swirled and spotted pane of glass. But the place where he'd stood was empty now.

I got back under the blanket, telling myself not to pay any more mind to dreams of white-haired boys. But sleep wouldn't come for a long time, and my chores the next morning seemed a far piece harder than they'd been the day before.

Chapter 21

I WAS SPLITTING A LOG OF BEECH WOOD FOR KINDLING when Noel came around. My hatchet broke the wood easily. There were no twists or knots in it. I stood a piece up on the splitting stump, took aim, and brought the hatchet blade down. The wood came in two with a satisfying pop.

"I brought you something," Noel said. I didn't look up from my work. "Look."

I took aim and cracked down hard with my hatchet. The two split pieces flew apart.

"Look," he said and thrust out his hand. It was a small square of something wrapped in greasy paper.

"What is it?" I asked.

"Open it."

"Why are you giving me something?"

"It's a present. Open it." He looked over his shoulder, as tho afraid his brother might be watching.

I split the stick of wood one more time, stacked the pieces, and only then took the little present.

I unwrapped it and found a small, light brown square. "What's this for?"

"It's maple sugar. It's sweet. You eat it and it tastes good."

"I know what's maple sugar. But how come you give it to me?"

He told me to try it and I did, nibbling at a corner. It melted on my tongue like butter but had that warm, sweet savor of maple syrup. "What's it for?" I asked again.

He was quiet awhile, then said, "I'm not as bad as I look. I take a bath and shave and comb my hair, and I can be a fair presentable man."

I put the rest of the maple sugar in my apron pocket.

"Leon will tell you I'm a dirty, drunken scoundrel. He'll say anything to make me look bad. But it's not true. Not all of it."

"I got work to do," I said. I wanted no man-brutes talking like fools around me.

"Leon will say anything. I just want you to know I'm not so bad." And with that he slunk back to his work.

At supper the brothers argued terrible, and I was afraid they'd take to each other with knives right there. Their arguments were never about anything much, which way to run a plow furrow, who forgot to milk the cow, talking too much at the dinner table. But from the way they went at it, you'd have thought they were fighting over a big pile of pirate gold. They'd curse and accuse each other of all sorts of mischief and say the other one was no better than fly droppings.

That night, while they fought, I took my plate and ate quickly by the hearth. Then, thinking one was going to grab an ax and go at the other like a butcher, I went to my room and fixed the door shut.

Finally the sun was down, and they managed to finish their fight without killing each other. I snuck out to clean up the pots and plates and ground a little corn for the next morning's mush.

Chapter 22

I DIDN'T GO TO BED DIRECT THAT NIGHT. WHEN I was sure the brothers were asleep, I snuck out and hid in the shadows of the smokehouse.

It was cold and cramped, but still I think I dozed some. Then, when the moon was out, just a tiny sliver of it, I saw the boy. He came turning and swaying over the grass, and I could see he was looking toward my window.

He went closer, seeing that the glass was empty. I stood up and whispered, "Hey."

"Hey yourself," he said, turning to face me. His voice wasn't crackly and low like other boys my age. He spoke smooth as the wind. He was a little taller than me, and it appeared he hadn't had to shave yet. But I wasn't so sure how old he really was. Depending on how you looked at him, he might have been ten years old or a hundred.

"Who are you?" I said.

"I should ask you the same exact question."

It was strange how he stared at me, as if I were a blurry looking glass and he was searching for his own face there. That's not to say we had any resemblance. It was more that by seeing him, I was saying, "Yes, you're really and truly somebody, not just some flicker of moonlight."

"I work here now," I said. "My pa sold me for a serving wench. I got three hundred and sixty-one days left, and then I go home." I waited for him to talk, but he just stood there regarding me with that sad, yearning look.

"Were you looking for me tonight?" I asked.

His reddish pink eyes went toward my window, and I followed them. In that light, the little round pane might have been a looking glass, reflecting the star-strewn sky.

"Why do you come here at night?"

He said the sun hurt his eyes and burnt his skin. So he had to go about in the dark.

"You live here?"

"Hereabouts." He pointed with his thumb back toward the woods. The great birch trees were the same color as he was, and I fancied for a moment that he was born from them, a kind of forest spirit.

He took my hand, and it was as cool as a night breeze. "Do you got a name?" he asked.

"Of course. Who doesn't have a name?" He winced a little at this, and I brought my voice down lower. "Hannah Renner. Backward and forward."

He didn't understand that, and I explained about my pa's looking-glass words.

"You can call me Brother Boy."

"That's your real name?"

"It'll do." He let go of my grip and brought his hands to his face, sniffing. His smile was lopsided, almost like it hurt to be happy.

I asked him if he had folks around there and a house to live in.

"My ma and pa are not of this world no more." Most boys would say that with sadness or grief or mayhap a little prayer. But he told me this the way he'd say it were going to rain. "I live just all by myself."

I didn't know what else to ask, and he didn't seem to want to talk anymore. But he stayed there, looking at me. It was quiet a long time, and we stood together in the dewy grass as tho neither of us could decide which one was dreaming and which was the dream.

Finally I asked if he didn't get lonesome out in the woods all by himself.

He had no answer for that.

I told him I had to get up before the sun to fix the brothers their food.

"They're a couple of wild savages," he said. "Not much better than beasts."

"You know them?"

"All my life." He pointed to the corn crib and the smokehouse and then to the kitchen garden. "I feed pretty well off their labors."

"And they don't know about you?"

He didn't answer. A sour, sighing look came on his face.

I said maybe we should move farther away from the house so we didn't wake the brothers.

"You could dance a reel on the roof, pounding with a rifle butt to keep time, and they wouldn't wake up. When they fall asleep, they're like bears in their winter cave."

He pointed up at the sky, toward that cluster of stars my pa called the Big Dipper. "You know some folks see that as a bear. I don't. I never could see it. Looks more like a snake with a great swollen head to me."

Tilting my head back and gazing up at the sky made me realize how bone tired I was that night. I started to sway a little. Brother Boy put his hand on my shoulder to steady me, and said, "You best get to your bed."

"You'll come back tomorrow?" I asked him.

"Or the next night. I'll be here."

With that, we took the parting hand and he was gone. I stood there awhile in the cold light of the stars wondering if Brother Boy would really return. Then I finally decided there was no telling but to wait and see. So I went back to bed and was asleep as fast as shutting a door.

Chapter 23

THE NEXT DAY MY CHORES WERE BOTH LIGHTER AND a power more heavy. Not getting enough sleep made me drag around. And the brothers took turns pointing out how slow and lazy I was that day. But their corn mush cooked up fine and the salt pork didn't burn, and they were soon off to their work.

My labors were easier because I could stop now and then and think about my visitor of the previous night. Tossing out the wash slops, I made a point to wander around the place where Brother Boy and I had stood. And yes, there were two sets of footprints.

I worked the garden and wondered if he'd come to steal my greens. And I decided that I wouldn't mind. By the look of him, it didn't seem he ate too much.

About noontime I went to my room and found the little half chunk of maple candy I had left. I nibbled one corner and wrapped the rest up, thinking that Brother Boy might never have tasted such a delight.

Then it was back to splitting wood, hauling water, and finally getting at the great spinning wheel, which I hated most of all. But I'd only done a few turns, hardly a handful, when Noel came in and told me to lay my work aside.

"Set down there," he said. I did as I was told. "You can take a little rest if you like."

Only then did I see that he had a bleeding wound on his forehead. He dabbed it with a rag. I asked what had happened. "That Leon's got a temper on him like a whirlwind. I told him he had the ox traces tangled, and he chucked a rock of flint at my head. But I fixed him good." He showed me his fist; the knuckles were all scraped raw. Then he said he'd have to collect some spider web in the barn to stop the bleeding.

He got up and said, "You take a little rest if you like."

I thanked him, tho I didn't comprehend why he'd growl and bellow at me when his brother was around and talk almost civil when we were alone. He left, and I sat a while staring at the spinning wheel as tho by just the power of looking I could make it turn.

I drifted off to sleep with my head down on the eating table.

Chapter 24

THE BROTHERS' STRIFE ENDED EARLY THAT NIGHT. SO I got to bed and was dead to the world when the sun was not quite gone. If Brother Boy came, I didn't hear him.

The next day was Sunday, and I announced in no doubtful terms that I didn't work on the Lord's Day. Other than making their breakfast, I was free. They glowered and sputtered a bit, but it was clear I was not going to listen to any argument.

So I set off for home well before noontime.

Having worked constant for a week, this free time felt peculiar. No one would shout orders nor complaints. No one would be watching over me to see my mistakes.

The walk home was a long but happy one. I dawdled a little while crossing Gat's Creek. Spring runoff had swollen the stream, and it played a bright music splashing on the rocks. The world seemed greener, and the sun warmer, the farther

I got from the Barrows' place. All the great trees were leafing out, and within a week there'd be a thick canopy shading the path I walked along.

I even sang a while, one of the songs I'd learned from my new book.

> How long Dear Savior O how long
> shall this bright hour delay?
> Fly swiftly round ye wheels of time
> and bring the promised day.

I knew that folks sang that song about the Lord's return, when he'd come from the sky in glory. But as I walked along toward home, I sang about a lesser day of deliverance. In a year, less a week, I'd celebrate my promised day.

As I went, even my wrath toward Pa waned. He'd been a fool. He'd always be a fool, I supposed. But he was still my pa, and I couldn't remain angry forever.

I called out when I got to the cabin. But he wasn't there. I looked inside and felt a sharp clutch of longing. It was smaller than the Barrows' and dirtier and had no windows to speak of, but it was still my home.

The ashes in the hearth were cold. The big iron frying pan was scummed with grease that looked a week old. Pa's cider jug sat open and empty. I was afraid then, afraid that he'd given up eating for liquor.

His bed was a tangled mess. But unless I straightened it up, it always was that way. I called out again for him. Silence was the only answer.

I went out to the shed and found that Mim was gone. Perhaps Pa had ridden her into town or was traveling around the woods with his new amulet. But then the thought struck me he might have sold her too.

"Pa! It's me, Hannah!" I shouted. My voice echoed in the trees and died.

I'd hoped for a happy homecoming and found myself lonelier than ever. Now I regretted flailing Pa so sharply with my tongue the other day. Perhaps he'd abandoned our cabin and might never visit me at the Barrows'.

With only the vaguest notion of where I was headed, I set off. The sun was still bright and the air warm, but no more song came from my lips.

I followed the trace to the Genesee and sat awhile watching the river flow. Logs and spring wreckage moved northward. In a week or so they'd tumble over the falls at Rochester and then float out into the huge lake I'd never seen. It occurred to me that I might make myself a raft and flee that place forever.

If my pa was gone, what should hold me there? It would be a hard life in a big city. I'd have to scrimp and slave. But how would that be any different from toiling for Leon and Noel? I could clear all the food out of the cabin, lash a few logs together, and sail northward. Just before the falls, I'd hop off my little raft and start a new life.

I could even choose a new name, I thought. I could make myself up new, like a storyteller making a tale out of wind and fancy and the scrap ends of dreams.

"But this is where I live," I said out loud to the river. "This is my home."

Only fifty-one more weeks and I'd be free again.

I got up and headed back. But I took a path through the woods I seldom followed, then split off from it and went with just the sun to guide by.

No ax had touched these trees. So most were huge around and had folded, knobby bark. The light seeped down from the treetops thin as cobwebs. The ground was oozy, sucking at my feet as if to draw me into the earth.

A thought blew a little breath on the coals of my hope. I could run off to this place, or one even deeper into the woods. I could disappear and make a life of solitude. Sitting down, I studied the woods and wondered if I might live on what the earth provided.

And then my mind wandered back to the night previous. I thought on Brother Boy and wondered what he ate and where he slept and how he kept warm through the winter.

Soon I shook these thoughts off. For who would take care of Pa when he got old? And who would take care of me in my timeworn days?

I set off again, heading deeper into the ancient forest. Following a ridgeline, I skirted a deep black pond. It was round as a kettle and ringed with tall hemlocks. No wind was moving that I could detect, yet the surface of the pond stirred. I stopped to watch. The surface calmed. I took a few steps, and again I saw tiny outward-moving ripples.

Something lived down in the depths, hidden. Its world was black, day and night. Still, I thought, it had a home and was safe there.

I traveled on a while longer, till I came to the ruins of a shelter. The hewn log beams were crusted with green moss. The stones of a hearth were toppled in a heap. To one side was a small clearing, perhaps where a garden had been.

A few spears of afternoon light stabbed down from heaven. And I thought, Here's a place where I might make my home.

Who had lived there before? It might have been a hunting camp. Or perhaps a family had tried to live there but given up. It didn't have the look of a Seneca dwelling. But I'd heard of some Indians who'd married white folks and set up a kind of half-civilized life in the woods.

Whatever the case, the people were long gone.

I pried a few boards and was jolted back by a fierce growl. There in the shadows were four angry eyes. Then came the twin squeals of two furious pigs. I retreated as tho the noise were a whip of knotty rawhide.

And then the two ruddy duroc brutes emerged from their lair. They were huge, lumbering toward me shoulder to shoulder, their mouths gaping to show gnarled pink-black tongues. Their wet snouts stabbed at me like a pair of fists. And their awful snorting beat the air as the dasher churns buttermilk.

I'd seen a great boar pig kill a dog in a wild frenzy. It took the cur by a leg and shook him like an angry girl child might shake her corncob doll. Then it tossed the dog through the air. And when he landed, it bit him to death.

So I knew that when full-grown pigs let loose their squealing war cries, it was no play-acting.

I talked soothing and placid to the pigs, for I knew that I could not outrun them if I bolted. They calmed a small measure but still fixed me with their tiny black eyes.

"There's a good fellow," I cooed. I'm certain they heard the fear in my voice. "There's a pretty pig."

At last their fearsome grunts quieted. I backed up a few steps, still prattling to them as if they were sleepy babes. "You go back to your little house," I said. "Go on. I won't disturb you no more." I put more distance between us, and they turned their attention to what acorns and beechnuts might have fallen while they had slept.

Soon I was well away from the pigs' lair. It took a long while more walking before my breathing finally calmed.

Fleeing the pigs, I'd given no thought to direction. And

now it seemed I was lost. Clouds had come in with the sun's descent, and so I could only guess at which way lay back to the Barrows'. I felt for the wind, which usually comes from the west, but under the thick canopy of trees, the air was still. I closed my eyes and stretched out my hands, as if I might receive a message from the sky.

Chapter 25

THO LOST, I FELT NO PANIC. FOR I COULD CERTAINLY live a day or three in the woods. I knew I could find a stream and follow it down to the river and from there retrace my steps.

My fear was what the brothers would think, and do, with me gone. Would they declare my contract broken and add another month of slavery for every day I was gone? Would they go after my pa and take their vengeance out on him?

At the least they'd say I'd abused my Lord's Day privileges and could no more wander, even when I should have the freedom to do so.

I surely needed to return. I had to be back cooking their breakfast and ready to labor before the sun rose.

But which way? I walked a short distance to a clearing, then craned my neck back and looked straight into the cloudy sky. The gray fleece was moving. So, guessing that it was heading toward the east, I set my course and hurried.

The ground was hilly, broken with great boulders of rock. It would be years, perhaps decades, before someone cut these trees, for the ground would never submit to the plow or harrow.

The hemlocks gave way to maples. Soon I saw a welcome sight: little spouts poking from the trees' bark. Someone was tapping maple sap here. And so, I told myself, I would soon find a path.

Buckets were placed under the dripping spiles. I thought it was a bit early to be collecting sap. But inspecting the buckets, I found some had a fine harvest. I was hungry. So I used a leaf stem to pick out the dead flies and fallen grit and had myself a long drink. In that form, not boiled down, you can barely taste the sweetness of the sap. But when I closed my eyes and thought on it, I detected a faint maply savor.

I placed the bucket back in its spot, just in time for another pale drop to fall from the tip of the spile. Then I drank from another and another bucket, wending my way through the sugar bush.

Still, I found no path. The way I'd seen the sap collected, folks used a sled with a great barrel on it. But perhaps this sugar man wore a yoke on his shoulders and backed the sap to his boiling place.

With my stomach full, and more sure that I'd soon find my way back, I felt a sleepy calmness descend. Surely, I could take a little nap and still be back to the brothers' farmstead before the sun was down.

So, with heavy footsteps and drooping eyelids, I looked for a likely place.

A low, shrubby tangle met my eye. It had an opening, like the mouth of a small cave. I poked my head inside and saw that some forest beast had used this place for shelter. I'd seen other spots with the grass packed down by a doe and her young fawns. Thinking she wouldn't mind my using her bower for a short time, I laid myself down. The spot was soft with leaves. And the low arching cover gave it the feel of a rich girl's bed, surrounded on all sides by brocaded curtains.

I slept. I woke in the deepest darkness. At first I had no idea where I was, but hearing the rustle of leaves as I moved, I remembered.

A misty spot, somewhat less black, hung before me. This was the doorway. I scrambled out on my hands and knees. It was pitchy black night, and I had no idea how to get back.

Chapter 26

THE MOON WAS GONE, AND FOR THAT I FELT ALL THE more forlorn. It might seem peculiar, but since I was a little girl, I'd thought of the moon as my friend. When Pa was addled with drink, when our corn and salt pork were almost gone, when others pointed and whispered about me, still the moon was there. Constant and true, I could depend on her.

But this night there was only blackness as thick as the tar they use to waterproof boats. And a silence as deep as the grave. No wind sighed in the treetops. I heard not even the moaning hoot of a far-off owl.

As a mind will in lead-heavy darkness, my thoughts traveled down dire paths. Tho most of the Seneca were gone from our territory, still, I knew, a few remained. Solitary and hidden, crazed by the loss of their land, wouldn't they pounce on me to take their vengeance? And runaway law breakers too were said to travel there, fleeing from justice. Pa had seen a fellow hanged at Little Sion. This was before

I was born, but still there were desperate men about. And perhaps worst of all were the rattler snakes that slithered among the rocky places. We didn't see many anymore. But just the year past Willy Bolcom had caught one with a forked stick and brought it back to town in a tow sack. He'd kept it for days in a disused whiskey barrel, and I'd paid a penny to see Willy toss a frog in and watch the serpent swallow it up.

With those thoughts plaguing me, every low rattle seemed a lurking threat. I stopped, listened, took a few steps, stopped again.

Overhead, great elms and chestnuts raised their arms like worshipers in some night-black church. I listened again, and the silence was vast and hollow. I knew tears would do me no good, nor sniveling, as my pa called it. But my fear was too much to be borne. This was my punishment, I told myself. I should have stayed at the Barrows', toiling even on the Lord's Day. I had no right to freedom. And this judgment, crushing me as sure as boulders can crush a worm, was my reward.

It was sheer folly, I knew, but with a shaky voice, I began to sing. If I wanted to draw Indian warriors or desperadoes to me, there'd be no better way. Still, I sang on, to push back the black silence.

My spirit looks to God alone
My rock and refuge is His throne.

It was a song I'd learned from *Wyeth's Repository*. It was sad, a minor-key tune, but I liked the words.

> When helpers fail and foes invade
> God is our all-sufficient aid.

My voice dwindled down to almost nothing. Yet I kept on singing.

> Trust Him, ye saints in all your ways,
> pour out your hearts before His face.

I heard footsteps coming and knew as sure as I knew my own name that I was doomed. I sniffed and wiped my nose on my sleeve, and thinking it better to face death with a song, I started up again.

> In all my fears, in all my straits
> my soul on His salvation waits.

Then I saw a reddish glow and thought that this was no Seneca who'd slit my throat but a very devil come to drag me to Hell. He loomed into view, slender as a whip but washed in crimson shadows. My voice rose, my only weapon. The preacher man, Mr. Dow, had said that Satan must flee from a holy song. So I sang. And the figure came toward me.

"You're a peculiar one," he said. The voice was no infernal boom but a soft lilt. "Out here all alone, singing." He laughed softly. "You are a very remarkable girl."

Then I saw it was Brother Boy and not a savage. My voice ceased, for the song had done its job. I was not to die that night.

He came near and squeezed my hand, to assure me all was right. When my tears had ceased, I told him why I was there and what had happened to me that day and night.

He blew on his little pine-knot torch, and it sputtered to brighter life. His skin was as pale as bleached canvas, and the torch's glow painted him redder than any Indian.

"You need to be back soon," he said. "Leon and Noel will mete out a horrid bad punishment if you're not back in time to make their breakfast."

And so we went, not in a straight line I think, back toward the Barrows'.

Chapter 27

THE NIGHT WAS NO LESS DARK, BUT WITH A GUIDE, MY fears were transformed. Now the somber army of trees, the hunched-up shoulders of rock, and the prattling creeks were no longer a threat. Brother Boy wandered this way and that. I'm sure even in daylight I could not have followed the trace. Our path was certain, however, leading me back.

"You might have asked before you took my maple water," he said as we came to a place where the trees were hung with buckets. "I would have gladly given you some." So I found out it was Brother Boy who tapped the trees to make the sweet syrup. Indeed, he had maple sugar with him then, a small cake of it which he gave me to eat.

We passed the little morsel back and forth as we walked. And so, the sweetness of maple juice and Brother Boy will always be linked in my mind. He had about him a liquid quality, as tho not made of earth like ordinary folk. When his time came to leave this world, I thought, he would not go back to clay and dust but rise like dew into the sky.

Coming to a grassy hillside, I got a fine view of the heavens. Still no moon, but now the stars poked their silvery lights through the welkin's blackness.

We stood there a long while, looking to the north. I made to set off, but he bade me stay. We waited, as tho expecting something from the sky. Again, I said I must return. Dawn was a short ways off and we had a long distance to travel yet. Again, he said no. Not harsh, like a taskmaster, but gentle, and almost sad, I thought.

So we stood on the hillside in a dreamy silence. I felt my legs growing weak. I wavered, and Brother Boy put his arm around my shoulder to steady me. Then it came.

At first I thought it was merely the blur of sleep. But I stood straighter, peered intently, and there were ghostly wavering lights. There was color to them, but I think not a color I'd ever seen. They turned and throbbed and roiled like a cloud of angry smoke. But so silent, so far away. At one point they looked like curtains buffeted in a breeze. Then they coiled in on themselves as a snake would. Moments later they'd dissolved and spread like the river's waves hitting a sandy shore.

"The northern lights," he said. "I've seen them these past few nights." Now the glow was pulsing like a bruise in the sky's flesh. "But this is the best they've been."

After watching a long while, I asked Brother Boy if he believed in ghosts.

"What kind of ghosts?"

The lights in the sky might have been spirits, I thought, spirits riding on wings of holy song to Heaven.

"Did you ever hear the story of the old Bible prophet called Elijah? He saw fiery wheels turning in the sky, the chariot of the Lord coming down. It was like a whirlwind of flames, rumbling and roaring. And it took him away on that wild midnight ride. And he was never seen again in this world. Free of pain and sorrow and human plight. Straight from here to Heaven with no death nor illness to vex him here." Why I said this, I didn't know for sure. But standing there with Brother Boy, I thought of fleeing this world and leaving no trace behind. "One time I heard a preacher man call that the wild ride to Heaven."

He was quiet a long time, then said, "My ma and pa have gone to the next world. But it was the fever that took them to their heavenly home."

"Their heavenly home," I repeated, staring at the beautiful lights.

Then we descended the hillside and struck off through the woods again. By this time I went like a sleepwalker. I was tired, but not just in my limbs from hard work. My thoughts were tired, lulled by the lights and the soft tread of our feet and by Brother Boy's presence.

However, as we wended along a rocky trace, I thought I heard far-off steps. I took Brother Boy's hand and told him to stop. Yes, indeed, there in the darkness were heavy plodding footfalls.

Leon and Noel, I thought. They've come searching for me in their wrath. I looked to Brother Boy. He said nothing, and his face was dimmed by the shadows. The sound came closer, heavier, like a great beast with anvils on his feet instead of hooves.

"What is it?" I whispered.

"Nebuchadnezzar and Melchizedek," he said. These names sounded like parts of a magic spell. He said them again, louder, calling out to the darkness.

Now my mind was a moil of fear. He's a demon, I thought, a demon of the night, and he is calling on his devilish cohorts. I turned back to flee down the trace. But he said, "Hold."

The pounding now was joined by a high-pitched whine, as though some infernal band of pipe and drums were marching toward us.

I broke from his grasp and ran. Brother Boy laughed, a soft, keening laugh. Then he called out again, "Nebuchadnezzar and Melchizedek!" and the two huge duroc pigs dove into sight.

One let out a twisted kind of squeal. The other grunted and moaned like thunder coming from underground.

Brother Boy went to them, scratched one behind the ears, and let the other lick his hand. Each pig was easily twice his size. When one reared back his head to let loose a wild snarling squeal, I could see a vast gaping mouth full of sharp teeth. With one bite, the pig could have taken Brother Boy's whole leg off. But they were at his command. They came at his beck and call, and they would obey him.

"This is Neb," he said. "And this is Mel."

They regarded me with their tiny red-black berry eyes. "Are they yours?" I asked.

"I watch over them, and they watch over me. They belong to no one. But I care for them when they need it. In winter, sometimes it's hard for them to find food. I claim a little from the nearby barns." He did not explain this any further, how a pair of monstrous pigs could keep watch over a boy.

He clapped his hands once and said, "Now go on! We need to be back soon." They turned and pressed into the underbrush. "You can make their acquaintance more fully another time," he said.

I was still quaking, my heart rapping in my chest like a hammer on thin slats of wood.

"We're not far now," he said and took my hand.

We went up. We went down. We went around a small tarn, the surface of the water black as the sky. We crossed a creek along a fallen log, like rope walkers at the circus. We passed through a glade of pines, and for the first time that night I heard wind moving in the treetops.

Then, of a sudden, we were in the Barrows' west hayfield. "You're back in time," he said. "My brothers will never know where you've been."

"Your brothers?" I asked.

"Noel and Leon. I'm the baby brother." With that, he gave my hand a quick squeeze and said his farewell.

He was gone the way the shine on a silver dollar goes when the light it reflects is snuffed out. I was alone there in the hayfield. No Brother Boy, no great lumbering pigs, no brilliance in the sky. Just a serving girl who needed to make breakfast soon.

Chapter 28

MY EXHAUSTION WAS LIKE A MILLSTONE AROUND MY neck. I drew water from the spring. I banked up the coals to make a cook fire. I mixed cornmeal and bacon fat for the brothers' mush.

I could barely make my limbs move. Yet I was not unhappy. I had a friend, I thought, as I went out back to split kindling. I might see him only at night, and only now and again. But he was a friend. He might be terrible odd and spend his time with monster pigs. But he was a friend, I told myself. And my year of servitude would not be so heavy if I knew I might pass some of my time with Brother Boy.

Leon emerged from his bedchamber first. Like a bear leaving his cave, his footfalls were heavy and his smell was dirty and sour. He sat at table and drank half a quart of cider in one draught. Then his older brother came to eat too.

"You were gone all day," Leon said.

I nodded, scraping mush into his bowl.

"We thought you broke the contract."

"I was at my pa's place." This was not entirely a lie.

He grunted in reply, shoveling food into his mouth. "No meat? Just mush today?" Getting no reply, he said, "We'll want sausage tomorrow morn. It should be ripe now. You slice down a few links and fry it up." I had my back to him. "Do you hear?"

"Yes," I said, hurrying to get the meal over with. They were odious to me, crude and bullying and never satisfied. Yet right then I was almost happy. As I rubbed the grease off the crockery and got water boiling for washing clothes, I told myself out loud, "You have a friend."

Going back into the house to get an armload of soiled clothes, I heard the brothers arguing. "No, not now," Leon snarled.

"The time has come," Noel replied, shaking his clenched fist. "There's no good in waiting." Then he turned to me. "Girl, come here."

"My name is Hannah," I said. "Call me by my name if you want me."

He scowled at my impertinence but said my name, bade me to sit at table with them.

"We didn't want to pledge ourselves to getting spliced without knowing exactly what kind of goods we'd get in the bargain," he began. "We thought it best to see how you work, watch how you do here."

I had no idea what he meant by this. But I knew it was bad news. I got up, saying, "I have a full day of chores. I best get to them."

"No," he commanded. "Sit." I stood my ground. "Take your seat." Seeing I would not back down, he softened his tone. But using words even halfway polite seemed to choke him. "Sit, if you please."

"I please to stand."

"Give the girl more time," Leon said.

"What's the good in that? We've seen she can cook and clean and do all the work a wife should do."

A cold, wet hand took hold of my heart. And then it squeezed. Again I made to leave. And again Noel bade me to stay. "We have important business with you, girl."

"She wants to be called by her name," Leon said.

The brothers glowered at each other like wrestlers ready for a killing match.

"Girl or Hannah, it's all the same." Then he turned to me. "We've been pondering on this all the while you've been staying with us here. And tho we might sound like we're in disagreement, it's all settled. A week's worth is enough to pass the test."

"What test?"

"You'll make a good wife," Noel said the way he might agree that a new mule would work well on the farm.

"Wife? I'm just a girl. You're not making any sense."

"Our ma was fourteen when she got spliced to our pa.

And he was already older than either of us now."

Leon addressed me directly for the first time that morning. "I want you to know I don't agree to this. We don't need no wife here."

"Wife?" I said in disbelief. "Wife? Whose wife?" My voice was faint as a far-distant wind. "I don't want to get married. I can't get married." I looked from brother to brother for some sign that this was a cruel joke or that perhaps I misunderstood.

"Girls your age are getting spliced already," Noel said. "I saw a girl in Little Sion, couldn't have been more than a year or two older than you, and she already had her first whelp. A boy child with a fierce black head of hair." His brother began to speak, but Noel told him to hush up. "And another set of hands would be terrible welcome in the field."

"I'm not getting married!" I shouted at them. "My pa won't let this be. You'll see!"

"Your pa done already signed the contract."

"He sold me to you for a wife?"

Noel nodded gravely, like a judge passing sentence on a lowly criminal.

With that I was gone, out, off beyond where their voices could reach to drag me back.

Chapter 29

I FLED. BUT WHERE WOULD I BE SAFE? MY PA HAD been off hunting his fool's treasure the day before. Besides, if the brothers were telling true, then Pa would give me no aid.

My second thought was to find Brother Boy. Yet I had seen him only by night. I had no idea where he laid his head for sleep.

Should I go to town? Who there would care to help the strange-eyed girl? They'd probably say it was fitting that I spend my days out there with the Barrows, a freakish girl with two freakish men.

Again I pictured myself on a little raft floating north on the Genesee's waters. I might make a life for myself as a serving girl in the city. Could that be any worse, I wondered, than spending my whole entire life with the Barrows?

Alone, trapped between bad and worse, I should have laid down and cried. But I didn't. I was powerful angry then. Lonely and forsaken, but full of rage.

I ran out past the stand of tall birches. Down a winding trace I went, running hard like one of those steam engines Pa talked about. Only I was burning my anger, not wood, for fuel. I stopped at Seven Creek and found a stout oak stick and began smashing it down into the water. I hit and I hit and I shouted at the silence, "I will not! I will not! I will not!"

Catching sight of a rock about the size of a man's head, and with two holes for eyes, I attacked it with new frenzy. I thought of that rock as Noel, then Leon, then my pa, then every man I'd ever known. I dashed the stick on the rock face until it broke into flinders. Then I grabbed up another one, but it was rotten and crumbled with my first blow.

Finally, I crumpled and knelt there with my eyes squeezed shut to keep in the tears. The brothers would not make me weep, I told myself. They would not wring one tear of grief from me.

When my heavy panting ceased, I stood up and set off. The fire yard, I told myself. It would be the best place for me. Pa was off chasing a golden ghost. I could have the place to myself.

I walked in a haze, seeing nothing but the path and my feet. I heard nothing but my own voice muttering, "I will not. I will not."

Chapter 30

REACHING THE BURNT, BLACKEN ACRES, MY HEART WAS dismally cheered. That was the place for me. There I could spend my days, in the habitation of old smoke and sodden ashes. There I would be unbothered by the folly of menfolk.

It appeared that my pa had not been there in many days. He'd given up honest work forever, I supposed.

I walked across the charred earth to his shanty. I went inside and lay down on Pa's sleeping tick. It rustled like a hundred snakes, tho I knew it was just oak leaves stuffed inside tow sacks. I lay there, and when my eyes grew used to the gloom, I spied a pile of books wrapped in oilskin.

If Pa could spend his days in idle thoughts and vain ponderings, then so could I. I untied the string on the oilskin and set to reading. The first book was full of strange etchings. I'd heard him rattle on about alchemy and anagrams and amulets. This book was of that sort. Truths of the natural world, but all twisted inside out and secret. I turned to the part Pa had underlined. "For it is most evident," I read, "that all beings have their equal and opposite. There can be no day without night to set its limits, no ocean without dry land to give it bounds, no cold winter without spring and autumn on either side and summertime to make the balance. Just so are we mortal creatures each of us surrounded by others who give our lives their shape."

The next book was more understandable. I'd barely read a page, however, when I heard the tread of feet.

My first thought was of the Barrow brothers, come to hunt me down like a runaway farm beast. But these steps were too light for Leon or Noel. Then I thought, It's Brother Boy. My new friend has come to give his aid and comfort.

I crawled out of the shanty.

"Daughter! Look here. Daughter, I told you I'd find treasure!" It was Pa, and he carried something long and thin and white.

He didn't ask why I was there, nor inquire about my health or happiness. He just shouted how he'd finally found what he'd been looking for.

"Look. Look close, daughter." He held out his treasure.

"It's an old bone, Pa. It's nothing," I said. I'd seen him scatter-witted before, completely caught up in his searches. I'd seen him pulled in on himself like a snail, so shut up in his thoughts that he couldn't hear me from two paces away. But never before that day would I have said he'd truly taken leave of his senses. "It's just an old leg bone. From a deer or a bear."

"No, look close." He held it out. It was indeed a specially long bone, with no breaks nor chips. But it was certainly not gold or ivory. He pointed to a pattern of scratches that ran up and down the bone. "You see? It's in cipher. If I can untangle the secret, then it will tell me where the treasure is hid."

I inspected the bone, and truly the scratches did look like a kind of writing. "But it's not in English, Pa. You can't tell what it says. Why do you think it's about treasure?"

He ignored this question, moving his fingertip along the rows of strange, crooked characters. "It's from the people who lived in this place before the Iroquois. The ancient folks who built great cities and temples. It'll tell me where to dig. I'm sure of it as I'm sure I'm standing here."

"Pa," I said, almost pleading. "Put that down for a bit and listen to me. The Barrow brothers said this morning they want to marry me."

He kept studying the bone, holding it only an inch or two from his eyes.

"Listen, Pa, this is terrible. I can't live there. I can't work there. They're talking about marrying me. Pa, this can't be. You won't let it, will you?"

I tried to grab the bone, but he shooed me away.

I was almost shouting now, but he didn't seem to hear. "They're talking about marrying, Pa. They want to marry me."

"Hmmm? Who's that?"

"Noel and Leon."

"Noel and Leon," he said. "Leon and Noel." Then his eyes lit up, and he grabbed me to plant a big kiss on my cheek. "That's it! That's it, Hannah. Backward and forward." He flipped the bone from end to end. "Exactly! The same coming and going, just like your name. Like Noel and Leon." He looked more carefully at the writing, turned the bone again, and nodded. "You're right. It's all in looking-glass characters. It's the same if you read it from either end."

"Pa, why won't you listen to me?"

"I am listening, Hannah. I always listen, but I don't always hear what you want me to hear." He was quiet awhile, trying to decipher the writing. Then he stopped suddenly and said, "Your eyes, daughter. Your eyes are like no others, and so they can see what I can't."

He'd told me once about Joe Smith the prophet man, how he'd translated his entire Golden Bible with special eyeglasses he peered through. They weren't like others tho, because each side was a different color from its mate.

"Look close, Hannah." He thrust the bone at me. "Shut the other one and look here with your green eye." As far back as I could remember, Pa had said that my one green eye was the special one. He said that with my milky eye closed, I was as pretty as an Ireland fairy. He also claimed, sometimes, that I had the gift of second sight. But I had no time nor patience for such foolishness that day.

I tried once more to make him listen. "Pa, they want to marry me." But he just jabbed the bone in the air and muttered about "Seeing through the secret."

With that I gave up. He was bereft of his senses, mad from greed, and could not truly hear a word I said. I was not a girl, not his daughter, just a strange pair of mismatched eyes he thought might bring him treasure.

So I ran again. He called as I fled. But I ran swiftly, and soon his voice was gone.

☾ Chapter 31

THOSE FOLLOWING HOURS ARE AS DIM AS DUSK IN MY memory. I suppose I wandered this way and that. I think at one point I heard Leon and Noel thrashing around in the woods, shouting my name. I felt like a slave girl who had escaped from her masters. I'd heard the preacher talk about those poor colored folks who were more lonesome and grieved even than the Jews enslaved in Egypt. At least the Jews, once they got their freedom, could walk back to their country. But the black folk had a vast ocean between them and their homes.

That was what I felt. A huge ocean lay between me and being happy.

So I wandered and pondered, and my thoughts went back to the fire yard. And my mind dwelt on the old Bible story of Gehenna. Like the old-time heathen people, my own pa had given me for a sacrifice. There was an evil god called

Moloch. And people would give up their own children for a burnt offering to him.

That time when the Reverend Dow had boarded with us, he'd talked about this awful pagan god. He found the place in his Bible and had me read the story out loud. Pa wanted to show off how good he'd taught me to read, bragging as if I was a trained monkey. But the Reverend Dow didn't care a twig about such things. He just wanted to preach the gospel. And he'd use whatever story he had to hand if it would help him make his point.

So there I was wandering, thinking on the fires of Gehenna and how grievous it was to be given away by your own pa.

When the last of the sunset had dripped out of the sky, I headed toward the Barrows' place. I hid in amongst the great birches till the brothers' candles were snuffed and the house lay in a heavy slough of darkness.

Then I waited longer. My hunger gnawed at my belly like a terrible worm. The growling had ceased at about sunset, but the pain continued.

Still I waited, till I was sure that the brothers were deep asleep.

Finally, I rose from my leafy hiding place and made my way toward the house. What was my plan? I'm not sure I knew at first. But once I'd eased the door open and seen the glow of the fire, it was clear.

I went as quiet as a shadow into the main room and stood staring at the coals. I could burn their house down, I told myself. I could turn all their work to smolder and ash. Then they'd need no wife. They'd pack their things and trek out farther west. And I might be free.

I took the biggest iron fry pan off its hook on the wall and squatted by the fireplace. I listened close. Yes, there was the twin whine of the brothers' snoring, like two saws struggling in a wet log. I blew on the coals, and they warmed, brightened. I blew again, and the smoke scratched my throat.

I had to cough. But I fought the urge. The hot itch grew and grew. And I fought it down by angry willpower.

I listened again. There'd been no change in the noise of the brothers' sleep.

So I scooped the skillet into the coals. Then I stood and carried the pan to the room that had been mine for a week. The door was open. Trailing a streamer of smoke, I went into the room.

Looking out the window at the birches, I thought I saw movement. But no, Brother Boy would not be there tonight, I told myself. I was alone, totally alone, and must do this dire deed all by myself.

The smoke wafted from the fry pan. I felt the handle getting warmer. I turned and looked at the bed where I'd laid my head that past week. Then one more glance out the window. I'll never have that view again, I told myself. When the house comes down in fiery crashes, the beautiful little window will be destroyed.

A streak of moonlight spread itself across the pasture. Then clouds churned past, and it was gone.

I puffed once on my coals and felt their warmth on my face.

Back in the main room, I considered how best to set the place on fire. First the tinderbox, then the pile of kindling, then the stack of firewood I'd cut two days earlier. I could move the chairs close to the blaze so they'd catch quick.

It would be easy. Once the blaze was roaring, I'd call out the alarm. I had no desire for Leon nor Noel to die there. I merely wanted to be free. With no house, no farmstead, they'd have no choice but to leave.

The corncrib first, I told myself. Burn the feed and they'd have to move on to keep the animals alive. So I left the house and went the short distance to the corncrib. This would go up like a torch. A few coals on the dry shucks, a puff of air, and the crib would be wrapt in flames.

So I readied myself. Do you want your freedom? I asked myself. "Yes," I said out loud. "Then do it. Then set the blaze."

I looked back at the house. Set the corncrib on fire, get the barn blazing, then get to work on the house.

"Go on," I said as tho talking to some other girl, someone not me who could do such a thing. "Set it on fire."

The hand that held the pan was hot now, shaking. The coals glimmered red and orange. I blew on them again. "Do you want your freedom?" I whispered to myself. "Yes." Still I couldn't do it. What would the cows eat come winter when the grass was all gone?

With that, I thought of my own belly, empty of all but pain.

What would I eat tomorrow? Freedom would not fill my stomach. "I don't care," I said loudly. Perhaps I wanted to wake the brothers so they'd keep me from such an awful deed. "I don't care!" I shouted.

Then the silence flooded back again. A tiny finger of smoke wriggled from the pile of coals. It rose, grew as thin as a thread, and disappeared.

"Go on with it," I said.

With my free hand I pulled a corn shuck from the pile and laid it on the pan of coals. It smoked for a moment, then curled and twisted as the bright flames consumed it.

It looked like something in terrible pain, writhing. Then it was gone, a black wisp caught and blown away by a little breeze. If I started this blaze, I told myself, then I'd be no better than those ancient heathens who burnt their own children as offerings.

"Do you want to be free?" I asked one last time. Then I cocked my hand back, and with all my strength, I tossed the whole pan of coals.

The crimson spray flew through the night air. The coals

glowed brighter, like a swarm of burning bees. They went in an arc, spreading out, hissing in the darkness.

And they landed in the dewy grass.

I had turned away from the crib before my throw. The coals lay in a glowing carpet on the ground. Some winked, some throbbed, some shivered. But they were all dying there in the evening damp.

"I knew you wouldn't do it." At first I thought the voice was my own. "I knew it." It was Brother Boy. He stood back in the shadows.

"I can't," I said. But what did I mean? Burn the house down? Serve as the brothers' slave? Enter into marriage? All of these, and something more.

"I can't." And then the tears that I swore I would not cry came free as rain.

Brother Boy stood with me as I wept. He let me squeeze his hand tight as I cried. We watched the last of the coals fade to nothing.

Then we turned away, and he led me into the darkness of the woods.

Chapter 32

WE HADN'T GONE FAR WHEN I REMEMBERED THE song book. I told Brother Boy to wait and ran back down the trace.

I'd left the door open. The coals in the hearth still pulsed with a warm red glow. I went quiet as I could past the fire and the kitchen and into my room. The book was under the bed, just where I'd left it.

Clutching it to my breast, I fled the house again, this time forever.

Back in the woods, I thought that Brother Boy had quit me. Worse, the thought came that he'd never been there at all. I'd seen him only in the nighttime. Neither Pa nor the brothers had ever mentioned him. Had I become as distracted from my senses as Pa? Was Brother Boy a kind of dream?

I stopped. There was no use in running if I had nowhere

to run to. I could call out but would as likely draw a panther or wolf as my friend.

Above me, where the treetops didn't quite reach each other, I saw the moon. It put me in mind of the looking glass and how once Pa had held it up to my face. One eye was like the moon—white and round, with faint blotches.

He'd rattled on that day about left and right and how one side reflects the other. "With the glass you can put away all that's uneven and see things square and true." He'd held the ragged piece of glass against the middle of my face, and it stuck out like a bright blade. He looked at my left side, doubled. "Two moon eyes," he whispered. Then he turned the glass around. "With the glass you become the same, just another green-eyed girl." But that seemed a bad thing to him. "There's right and wrong, man and woman, up and down, Heaven and Hell too I suppose. Everything has its twin. Left eye and right eye — you got to have both or you're not whole."

I craned my neck back and stared straight at the moon. If it was a great eye watching me, then was there another one?

The sound of a trembling whistle called me back to myself. I looked in the direction of the birdlike call, and there was Brother Boy.

"You came back," he said. "I thought you'd given me over."

"I wanted the book." I held it out to show him.

He came close, but by his look, I knew he could not read.

"It's called *Wyeth's Repository of Music*." I flipped it open and held the pages to catch a band of moonlight. The staves and notes and words were so much gibberish for him, like Chinese characters would be to me. "I'll teach you," I said.

He nodded and again we set off, down the winding benighted path.

Chapter 33

BROTHER BOY LIVED ONLY A FEW MILES FROM THE Barrows' house. But the woods there were as yet uncut, the creeks unbridged, the trails no better than deer paths. We went up and down rocky ridgelines, in and out of lonely dells.

The first pink of dawn was just smudging the eastern sky when we reached Brother Boy's abode.

Having slept not a wink that night, my feet could barely move, and my eyes could hardly hold themselves open. So he led me through a low doorway and had me lie down on a corn-shuck mattress. The air there was rank, like an animal's den. Before I'd drawn a half-dozen breaths, sleep took me.

Chapter 34

I THINK I DREAMED OF MY MA THAT NIGHT. SHE CAME to comfort me. In the dream she sat beside me and watched over me to keep me safe. But waking, she fled like mist burnt off by dawn's light. I'd dreamt of her before. And it was always a sore melancholy thing to wake and find that those feelings of solace were naught but night vapors.

More troublous was seeing where I'd fled to that night. I sat up on the hissing, crunching mattress and saw that I'd slept in a dank little shelter no better than a cave.

Brother Boy was not there. But a small shoat-pig was sleeping in one corner, and through the open doorway I saw robins and sparrows hunting in the grass. The sun beamed brilliant out there. And when the breeze picked up, it blew cleaner air into the hovel.

Next to the bed lay my breakfast. Three johnnycakes were stacked on a broken plate. And beside them was a flask made of hollowed-out cow horn. Now my hunger came like a panther's jaws biting me from the inside. I gnawed off a piece of corn crust, then drank to soften it. There was just enough cider to get all the hard cakes down.

I went outside. I soon learned that Brother Boy had built his home on the top of a hill. But the pines were so tall there, and grew so dense together, that at first I could see only a few paces around me. His home was a hodgepodge of huge stones, puncheon boards, poles with animal skins hung across, a piece of cloth he claimed came from a sailing ship, and strips of elm bark on the roof. Having just risen from a troubled sleep, I thought I might still be dreaming. I'd read in one of Pa's books about ancient beasts of fable, all cobbled together from parts of different animals. The head of a lion, the tail of a sheep, the claws of an eagle, the body of a bull. Brother Boy's den gave the same disordered feeling.

I walked around the crazy house and saw that he had one real window. A piece of glass not much bigger than the span of my hand was plastered into one wall. It looked out on the back of the house, giving a far view of the valley below.

A spring bubbled up not too distant from the house. I knelt there, brushed the pine needles away, and drank. Then I washed my face and washed it again. And I stood in a patch of sunlight to dry. With my eyes closed and the breeze coming soft and steady from the west, I was almost at peace.

Then I heard a gunshot, from far off. Maybe it was a boy from Black Stick hunting squirrels. Or a man killing a deer. Another shot rang out. It came from miles away. Still, it was a reminder. I could run, I could hide, but there were men who would hunt me down. Surely the Barrows knew where Brother Boy lived. Surely they'd come up there with guns as if I were a wolf who'd preyed once too often on their livestock.

I heard the grunt and squeal of Brother Boy's great pigs. Then I felt the ground shaking. They emerged, the three of them, from the pine shadows.

This was the first time I'd ever seen him by day. He stayed back from the bright rays of the sun, not hiding, but protected from the burning light.

He scratched one of the pigs behind his ears. The great beast made a rumbling, contented noise and squeezed his tiny eyes shut. The other one, jealous, nuzzled up to Brother Boy. "We're happy you're still here," Brother Boy said. "We thought mayhap you'd flee back to Gog and Magog when you woke."

"Gog and Magog? Where is that?"

"Not where, who. My brothers. The big boys. Your masters."

"What for do you call them that?" I'd heard it from the preacher, some names from prophecy. "And Gog and Magog shall rise up in the east."

"My given name is Redmond. Redmond James Barrow. But I call me Brother Boy. I find a new name for everyone I meet." He came across the patch of sunlit ground, squinting and wincing. Back in the shade, his pain lessened. "I call your pa the Muttering Man. And you're One Green Eye."

"My name is Hannah."

"True enough. But it's also One Green Eye."

Chapter 35

AND SO THAT WAS MY NAME WHILE I STAYED ON BROTHER Boy's hill. That first day he showed me his larder hole, where he kept apples packed with hay and sand. Then I saw his little sugar shack, with the great kettle he used to boil the maple sap. "That's all I got from my ma. Everything else Gog and Magog claimed. They let me take the kettle because they figured they'd get some of my sugar."

To stay out of the sunlight, we went along paths well shaded by the trees.

He took me to the creek that runs to the river. There we sat a while under a shelf of rock that jutted out like a roof. I asked him if he'd always lived by himself.

"Since my ma died. That's close on six years. That room you stayed in was mine, when I was a little one. My pa put the window in for me. I couldn't go out much by day. The sun makes me sick, weak and patchy and all red like a suckling pig over coals. I was no use on the farm. A half-hour, and I was like unto dying from the sun. So when my ma passed on, Gog and Magog said I was a burden, a useless mouth to feed. I told them I could learn a trade to ply indoors. Mayhap shoemaking or tinsmithing. But they just growled and murmured about me being like a worm in their bellies, eating and doing no useful work.

"So after a month or two of that, I went. And I don't think they even looked for me. I never heard them calling out my name. That's when I decided I needed a new one." We were quiet a long time.

There'd been fires made in that little shelter. The rock roof was black with soot. Bones and half-burnt sticks were scattered about. On one wall were strange markings. They looked old, ancient perhaps, carved into the stone. I crawled over to look. One was a head with big bulging eyes. Another looked like a rattler snake. The fangs were wide open, and the tail was raised to make its rustling alarm.

"There were people here before the Iroquois. Folks say they made those carvings. And the big blocks of stone for my house — they were there when I found the place. It was a kind of fort. I seen others around. Ruins, places the Seneca don't even know about."

"So then you already had a place to stay when you left your brothers' house?"

He shook his head. "First I just dug out a little hidey-hole not much better than a fox burrow. Lined it with oak leaves and spent a month lying in there by day. When the sun went down, I'd go exploring to find my true home."

I thought of my home. Might it fall to ruin without me there to take care of it? Pa wouldn't fix the roof or chink the walls, and in a short while rain and snow would be blowing inside. Then Pa would huddle in the fire-yard shanty with his books and amulets. Without me there to cook, he'd just eat parched corn like a farm beast. Without me to spin and sew, his clothes would fall to rags.

But how could I go back? The brothers would surely look for me there. "They told me they wanted to marry me," I said at last. Brother Boy knew who I meant. I found that he often could finish my thoughts, know my mind without hearing a word.

"Yes, that's why they hated me so. They wanted a girl in the house, a drudge wench. Not a boy who could do no honest work."

"I can't go back there," I said.

"Nor can I."

Chapter 36

THE SUN WENT BEHIND A HIGH IRON GRAY BANK OF clouds, and we made our way back to his den. Passing through a rocky dell, we were joined by Melchizedek and Nebuchadnezzar. They lumbered along, one on either side of us, like guards for a king and queen.

We passed by a huge old oak with some long poles propped against it like the skeleton of a tent. "I seen Old Crow here last year. He made his lean-to shelter there and spent the whole night praying out loud."

"Old Crow?" I asked.

"That's what I called him. Tall man in a raggedy black cloak. Big floppy-brimmed hat and eyes fierce as burning coals. It was raining hard, and I crouched just about here, listening to him. His praying would rise and fall, and I swear it sounded like a granddaddy crow screaming to the sky to gather up all his flock."

"Was it after harvest time?"

"Maybe. Can't remember when."

I told him it was the Reverend Lorenzo Dow, who'd stayed at our place for a few days. "He travels all over the country. He's even been to Ireland, he said, to preach."

One of the swine halted, sniffing. His eyes roved along the ground. And they both made snuffling grunts back and forth as if talking in the language of pigs.

The ground grew rougher, tumbles of great rocks strewn about. The pigs came in closer to us as we picked our way and talked about Reverend Dow and his camp meetings.

Suddenly the pigs reared back, squealing and snarling.

Brother Boy grabbed me by the arm. His eyes flashed this way and that, bright with alarm. "Rattlers," he whispered.

Then we heard the dry, buzzing noise that tells of killer snakes.

Melchizedek darted forward. Nebuchadnezzar let out a wild bellow, like a trumpeter leading the charge.

Brother Boy yanked me backward as the pigs lunged at the writhing nest of serpents.

The battle was like nothing I'd ever seen or read about. Screams of swinish rage struck my ears as the snakes poured from between the rocky crags.

I knew that pigs would eat anything and could hold their own in a battle with even a wolf. But the wildness of this combat was terrible to behold. Mel grabbed two snakes in his maw and flailed them like a whip against the rocks while Neb snapped his great jaws and sucked down the writhing severed parts. More than once a serpent would fasten its vicious fangs into one of the pigs' flesh, but the pig would rear back, biting fiercely and pulling the enemy's jaws away. Thick with fat, the pigs were safe from the rattler's venom.

I stumbled backward, away from the terrible affray. Brother Boy took up a stick and, using it like a sword, joined the combat.

Seeing that I was alone, one great serpent slithered from its cave and fixed me with glinting eyes. I stood still as granite. The snake came closer. It wanted me, wanted to sink its venomy fangs into my poor flesh.

As in a dream, I tried to move but was helpless to flee. I opened my mouth to cry for Brother Boy but no sound came.

A short distance away, the loud combat raged, horrible and awesome as the clash of ancient monsters. And there I stood as tho under a spell.

The serpent slithered close. It reared back its head as if aiming a spear point at my heart. At last I raised a hand, tho this was meager protection against this deadly king of vermin.

Its eyes shone yellowy gold. Its tongue flickered scarlet as blood. Its neck bulged as it reared to strike.

But like a nine-pound hammer falling on iron, hot from the forge, Nebuchadnezzar was on the snake. He bit clean through its neck. He spat the head to one side. While he sucked down the wriggling body, the head lay nearby, jaws snapping in helpless rage at the air.

Then the snarling was done, and the thrashing was over. Those few serpents that survived had all fled back to their dismal holes. Those which the pigs had killed were all gobbled up. And their bright slime shone on the rocks.

Brother Boy came to me. And I leaned, quaking, on his shoulder.

When my limbs had ceased their trembling, and when Brother Boy was sure it was safe to proceed, we made a quick path back to his shanty. Still loud with righteous fury, the pigs guarded us all the way home.

Chapter 37

THIS BATTLE, HE TOLD ME, WAS NOT THE FIRST TIME the pigs had stood between him and sure destruction. Only a few months earlier, two Iroquois brigands had tracked Brother Boy to his den and were set to take his life. But the two pigs had appeared like God's holy wrath, and the desperate Indian warriors had been sent fleeing.

We made a cook fire that night and feasted on corn and dried apples. The roof was too low for me to stand up straight. We sat together for a long while listening to the fire. Brother Boy said, "The flames talk, you know. The sound is words, but we just can't understand it."

I'd heard of folks who could make sense of the birds' singing or the far-off wail of wolves. But never had I thought that fire might speak too. "What is it saying?" I asked.

"I don't know. But when you're alone day and night for months, the sound of the flames becomes more of a comfort than human voices." We listened for a long time. Then of a sudden, Brother Boy crawled to the other side of the den and came back with a bundle wrapped in buckskin. He laid it on the floor, just before the fire, and showed me.

Inside were his treasures, all the things he'd found in his midnight wanderings. There was a rusty pistol and a broken knife blade. There were bits of old Indian pottery and a handful of bright turkey feathers. He showed me a scrap of paper with words on it and asked me to read it. But they weren't in English. He said he'd found it and the pistol in a camp down by the river. "Frenchmen came here long ago and burnt the Seneca's towns. I think the camp was from one of their scouting parties." Then he showed me a beaver pelt and a dried-up bear's claw.

But the treasure that was most precious was a great white tusk. "There were giants in the land, in the olden days. The Seneca tell tales of huge men who roamed this place. I think this is a tooth from a giant's mouth."

I held the great curved tusk in the firelight. Lines and crude little pictures were carved into it. It put me in mind of something I'd seen in one of Pa's books. In ancient days there were great elephants in this place. Not smooth-skinned ones like those in far-off India, but shaggy with fur. I'd seen an engraving in a book, and Pa had told me some things that the natural philosophers had puzzled out about the terrible beasts. They were called woolly mammoths and lived there in the days of the great ice.

"It's wonderful," I said. The letters written on the tusk were unlike those of English: spidery, twisted, and scrawly.

"A giant's tooth," he said again. And tho I knew better, I didn't tell him otherwise.

"Can you make out the writing?" he asked.

I shook my head but inspected the tusk closer. Tho the words were strange and blurry, with wandering curlicues, a few of the letters were familiar. "Here," I said, pointing to a character that might have been a capital *B*. "This is the same as in English." I circled my fingertip around the *B*. "This is the letter that begins your name. *B* for *Brother Boy*."

This drew him nearer. "Is my whole name there?"

"No, but here's a number 3. And this one's like an *H*, which is how you start my name."

I pointed to the *B* again and had him say it, almost humming it like a honeybee.

"Can you teach me to make the letters?" His voice was quieter then, with a pang of sadness in it. He took up a flat piece of birch bark and gave me a stick of charcoal from the hearth. I shaped two loops to make a *B* and then handed the stick to him. He tried. The letter shook and twisted, but it was indeed a *B*.

I put my hand on his, to guide him as he tried another one. "*B, B, B, B, B,*" he whispered as we wrote the letter again and again. "*B* and *B* and *B*."

Chapter 38

AND WITH THAT ONE LETTER LEARNED, HE SEEMED full of joy. *"Bumble bee,"* he said, practicing. *"Biscuits* and *butter."* He smiled at the thought of that. *"Bats* and *bluebirds* and *bears* and *bullfrogs!"* It made him happy to play at this, finding all the *B* words. "And we shall not forget *brave, bonny, Brother Boy."* He puffed up his chest and stuck out his chin. Then the laughter came.

I'd known how to read since I was little. I had no memory of the time when letters were new and strange. So teaching my friend was a double delight. For I could join him in his happiness and feel it for myself.

He prattled on with the words a while longer. Then he said we must go for a walk while the night was still fine.

We crawled out of the shanty and breathed in the cool darkness. Treetops swayed like old men in their sleep. There came a ceaseless sighing, the wind ruffling the high-up leaves.

It was well past midnight, I'm sure. Back at home Pa was

likely snoring away. I thought of the Barrows' house, dark and silent in sleep. And in Black Stick, and Little Sion and Dansville, and all the towns I knew of, people were deep in slumber. But I and Brother Boy were full, bright-eyed awake. And the woods, and all the sky we could gaze upon, were ours, just ours.

He led the way, down a trace so dark I might as well have kept my eyes closed. I went with my hand on his shoulder and never once tripped. Down to a place where I smelt water, the coolness of a spring reached us. Then upward we went, along a twisting sandy path where I got a glimmer of light above. This rising path seemed to go on forever. My feet were lagging and my breath was coming hard, when suddenly we were out in the open.

It was another hilltop, a high one. Spread out before us was a vast rolling landscape. The river meandered there, in loops and wriggles, heading away to the northern horizon.

"I think sometimes to build my house here," Brother Boy said. "If I hadn't already put so much labor into the other one, this is the spot I'd want to live."

It was indeed a wonderful place. I don't think I'd ever seen that far.

"On perfectly clear nights, with no clouds at all, I think I can see all the way to the great lake."

I was sure that if we inspected a map in my geography book, we'd find this impossible. But that night, I believed him.

"There's a shine out there to the far north, something

shimmery like low flames. But it's a cold fire," he said. "Way to the north, all is frozen."

"Mayhap it's light shining off the ice," I said.

He didn't answer, because the light, a faint glimmer, was there on the far-off horizon. "See?" he said at last. "You call its name and it comes." He took my hand, and we went to the edge of a steep cliff.

I saw a flicker to the north, then it faded. The emptiness stretched out below us. The tops of the biggest trees were so far down we could hardly make them out. A vast sea of darkness below, with the river winding its way to the lake. And far, far off were the wavering northern lights.

"Hello!" Brother Boy shouted. The noise jolted me, as a firm hand will jolt a sleeper to wakefulness. He shouted again, and we heard an echo.

"Go on," he said. "You call out."

But I wouldn't do it.

He shouted again, even louder. "Brave, bonny, Brother Boy!"

We waited, and then the ghostly voice came back to us.

The lights were stronger now, dancing like smoky specters. "You see? You call out and they come."

He let go of my hand. I felt woozy and weak, sleepy and yet more awake than I'd ever been. I backed away from the cliff edge, fearful I'd plummet, drawn into the dark air by the echoes and the shimmering lights.

Brother Boy went a short distance to a big tree with a hollow in the trunk. He took up a fat stick and hit it against the tree trunk. A heavy boom filled the air. I went back to the cliff edge and listened. He pounded his tree drum again, and I heard the sound echo back. Again he hit the tree. I wondered what it sounded like down there, miles away. Were sleepers troubled by the far-off steady thunder?

"You try it," he said, holding the stick out for me. But I said no. I looked to the north. I told him to hit again. He did, and I'm sure the lights quaked, as when you toss a pebble into a pond. He made the drum ring, and now the lights were fully alive.

I thought of a song I'd learned at camp meeting and sang it out.

> Elijah saw the fiery wheels turning in Heaven.
> He saw the chariot of the Lord burning in Heaven.

Brother Boy hit again, keeping time, one great ringing boom on every downbeat.

> Elijah saw the fiery whirlwind falling from Heaven.
> He heard the rumble and the thunder calling from Heaven.

And so it went, a girl singing into the blackness and a boy sending his low, booming drumbeat to the end of the world.

I got to the end of the song and sat down with my feet dangling over the cliff edge. The last drumbeat came back to us, and then all was silence. The northern lights unrolled themselves like a great scroll in the sky. I could not read the scroll but thought it must bear glad tidings.

Chapter 39

THE NEXT DAY, THE SUN WAS MUCH SPENT BY THE time we emerged from his little den. We headed down to the riverbank and sat awhile. I'd brought along my book, thinking I might show him the words to one of the songs.

"Here," I said. "This one is called Bridgewater." I said the words. Then I sang them for him. "Blessings abound where e'er he reigns. The pris'ner leaps to loose his chains."

"*B* for *Bridgewater*?" he asked. I nodded. "*B* for *blessings*?" He understood, and it gladdened my heart considerable to see him struggle with the words and triumph.

"*B* for *Brother Boy*!" he yelled. His words flew across the wide river and echoed back to us. Then he asked, "What letter is for *One Green Eye*?"

Should I show him the letter *O*? Or the number 1? At last I said, "*H* is for *Hannah*." I took up a splinter of shale and wrote my name on a flat rock. "You see? *H. A. N. N. A. H.* Either way backward or forward, it's the same."

I wrote "Don't nod" and pointed to the words. "That's another one. See — left to right or right to left it's the same." He couldn't read this of course, and I suppose I was showing off. "Here's the best one I know: 'Niagara — War Again.'"

This puzzled him greatly. I ran my finger under the words, first one way and then the other. Confusion darkened his look. Seeing his distress, I went back to his name. He took up my little writing stone and made looping *B*s, big as a shout.

Beyond the river, the sun was burning up its last fires. I've heard folks say that shadows fall. But that evening, I think they rose. The darkness seemed to come up from the earth. This was no terrible darkness, full of threat, but the shadow that blurs away all flaws and faults.

The river ran by, fat and full and lovely. The stars poked themselves like bright pins through the black velvet of Heaven. I sang, quiet as a mourning dove, songs I knew by heart.

At last, tho, came the time to leave. I said we should rub over all the letters he'd drawn. "We don't want to leave any sign we've been here."

"It matters naught," he said.

"We don't want your brothers to know where we are."

"They know," Brother Boy said, and I felt an icy claw tear at my heart. "Not exactly. But they'll find us soon enough."

Just those few words, and I heard an iron door slam shut like in the deepest prison. "They can't," I whispered. "Never. I won't go back to that house again."

"They came out a few times to the sugar bush and drank up a few quarts of my boiled sap. They have a rough idea where I am. And they want you back."

A silence fell between us, black and vast as the ocean.

"I can't go back there," I said. "I won't. Never."

"They've already come looking. Yesterday I saw their tracks. They move as clumsy as oxen, breaking branches, leaving footprints. They came close. They missed us, but they'll return."

Chapter 40

OUR TREK BACK TO HIS DEN WAS AWFUL. AT EVERY turn of the path, I listened for the sound of the Barrows' approach. "They won't come by night," Brother Boy said. "They need sunlight to find us. If we stay out of sight by day, it may take them weeks to catch us."

Weeks, days, months: what did it matter if it was certain they would find me?

We fell asleep not long before dawn. I woke a few times during that day, sure I heard the clumsy footfalls of Leon and Noel. I lay there on the corn-shuck mattress, trembling, praying that I'd be passed over, like the houses of the ancient Jews who were passed over by the angel of death. Each time, my frantic breathing did calm. Each time, the noises went away and sleep returned.

Then finally dusk was upon us, and I felt my terrors lift.

Brother Boy unwrapped a little cake of maple sugar.

He unstopped his cider flask and handed me a fine slice of venison steak he'd been roasting as I drifted up from my troublous slumbers. The cider had a heady tang and the sugar a strange sweetness. And so we dined like fairyland's royalty. His abode might have been as dark and low as a bear's den. But with the fire crackling and the food warming our bellies, we supped as happily as any wildwood nobles.

Darkness was well upon the land when we emerged from the den. A wind was moving in the treetops, not moaning like a ghost as it sometimes does, but sighing. Steady and pleasing to the ear, it sang an evening song.

"They won't come by night," I said, repeating Brother Boy's earlier words of assurance. "We're safe. We're free." At least until the sun came up again.

The night creatures spun their web of shadow sounds. Peepers down in the marshy places, owls hooting high in treetops, the rustle of the creeping fox, and the high whine of mosquitoes.

We walked a long time in the moonlight. We crested a hill, and down below us was the river, like a vast black snake. I told Brother Boy how I pictured myself riding a raft north, away to another life.

"It would be terrible," he said. "Bustle and noise and endless work. The city is like a prison, and you'd never escape."

"Dragged back to your brothers' house will be a prison too."

He couldn't argue that. Nor could he give me any assurance that it wouldn't come to pass.

"We can hide by day," he said quietly.

"You said they'd find us soon enough."

"Yes, they will." We stared down at the river. A short ways north, it bent in on itself, making a great loop. The moonlight was caught in this oxbow, bright and shimmering like polished steel.

"But tonight," he whispered, "we're safe."

We walked a short ways on and he said, "Here. Right in this spot. I found it here." We'd brought the great tusk along to draw other lost relics, as a magnetized nail will pull other nails to it. "I was digging roots for tea and saw the white tip poke out from the ground. I kept on, and there it was, waiting for me."

Pa always said that like draws like. Gold will lead to more gold. Until that day I would have said this was so much foolishness. But being with Brother Boy, everything seemed inside out and upside down. We went out by night and slept in the daytime. Terrible pigs were our best friends. A poor girl and a poorer boy could live like a king and queen.

So, I thought, maybe Pa's nonsense might even be true there. I saw where Brother Boy had found the tusk and set to work digging with a sharp stick. "There might be more here," I said. "Bones or teeth or mayhap even spears and jewels the ancient people had." It was just pretend, but it made up both happy to think of finding treasure.

I'd only dug a short time when we heard the grunts and rumbling of the two great pigs. Out of the shadows they came, one from the west and one from the east, as if pulled there by the scent of the torn earth. They went direct to where I was digging and snuffled in the dirt as tho they smelt some delicious food.

However, my efforts there were to no avail. Soon the pigs wandered out of sight. But we could still hear them, rooting and scuffling in the earth.

"My pa spends his day all the time looking for treasure. And here it is. He knows a man who might pay you a fair high price for the tooth and put it in his museum of curiosities. If you find more, you could sell them and be rich."

Lost in the darkness, one of the pigs snorted. In reply, the other one came lumbering out of the shadows. Brother Boy stood up, looking around. "What is it, Neb?" The pig sniffed at the hole, then followed the noise and was gone.

"I've seen the Muttering Man not far from here, looking and poking and cursing when he found nothing. I spied on him a few times, then came back at night to dig where he'd been. Can't find treasure by daylight. The sun's too hot, drives treasure deeper into ground."

Again we heard the pigs grunting back and forth, as tho discussing some plan. "Nebuchadnezzar!" Brother Boy shouted. "Melchizedek!" Holding the tusk in his arms, he might have been a wizard shouting spells into the darkness.

"What's wrong?" I hissed.

The wind had picked up. Above us the tree branches thrashed and flailed. Again we heard the low rumbling of the pigs. By the watery moonlight I saw a night owl circling. He'd spotted his prey and would soon swoop down for the kill. It was beautiful to witness, and terrible too.

I began to ask again what was wrong. But Brother Boy shushed me, grabbing me by the arm. We listened. There came the heavy crunch of the pigs moving over dry leaves. I heard a far-off scream. I looked up and the owl was gone. He'd fallen from the sky like an arrow.

Brother Boy guided me a few steps backward, into the cover of a great beech tree with drooping branches. He put his mouth close to my ear. "You're my friend," he whispered. "You'll always be my friend."

Then came the roar and snarl of the pigs. Two voices shouted back curses. Leon and Noel appeared, like living shadows pulling themselves free of the greater darkness. The pigs too came into view, snapping and growling. Noel carried a huge hammer and swung at the attackers, keeping them at bay. His brother had a rifle and hung back, trying to take aim. One of the pigs lunged, with a fearsome trumpeting snarl. And the brothers retreated.

Still, tho, they had a rifle, and the pigs knew how deadly this was. One of them darted through a patch of moonlight to make a side attack. The other backed up, crouching in the dirt to make a lower target.

"Shoot! Shoot!" Noel yelled at his brother. But before Leon could pull the trigger, Brother Boy had come out from his hiding place. "It's us you want, not the pigs," he said.

The rifle swung in our direction. I screamed. The pigs flung themselves forward. Brother Boy grabbed me by the arm. The rifle went off with an echoing crack. Leon shouted a curse. His brother replied with a fouler oath.

And we were off, dashing along the dark path.

Chapter 41

THE CHASE WAS MORE CONFUSED THAN A FEVERED dream. We ran, and the brothers ran after us, shouting like madmen. Up a winding trail we clambered, then bolted down a long rocky hillside. The pigs came and went like angels of death or perhaps devils of revenge. I'd never seen anything that big, that heavy, move so fast.

Brother Boy knew the paths best. But we were running, not skulking quietly along. And for such huge behemoths of men, Leon and Noel could keep up a fair pace too.

Running pell-mell across a meadowy path, we saw the brothers emerge behind us like two bloodthirsty he-bears. One grabbed the other, shouting. Then the first broke free and was after us again. Soon we were racing through a stand of birches, all glowing brilliant white, and then crossing a place of utter darkness.

We stopped to catch our wind. "They're gone," I gasped.

But then came the trumpet of the pigs, another gunshot, and we ran on again.

I remember our flight as I might remember pictures torn from a book and scattered in the wind. We passed twice, I'm sure, the same dell filled with nodding mandrake flowers. We splashed across a creek, and the water seemed like a looking glass broken into a hundred pieces. Black wings beat above us. I heard a hollow scream, perhaps a panther, perhaps a far-off echo of my own earlier scream. Then the pigs appeared, one of them smeared with blood. Brother Boy yanked harder on my hand and on we went.

There was the creek and the little cave where we'd whiled away an evening. Then came a ragged outcrop of granite, the crystals sparkling in the moonlight, and the black hulk of an oak that had been hit by lightning. The branches clawed at heaven, groaning in the wind.

Our pace slackened some as the brothers' noise grew fainter. I caught my breath enough to say, "Where are we going?"

Brother Boy said nothing. For there was no good answer. We could run all night and all day. We could hide and wander for weeks and months, but still there'd be no place of rest. I thought of the brothers fighting, growling their rage at each other. And then I understood why. Leon wanted me dead. I now saw that clearly. He hated me for the strife I'd brought into the house. If Noel did take a wife, then Leon's place would be as lowly as a servant's. He'd have no land, for the first brother always gained the father's inheritance. And the other one, Noel, wanted me back at the house, a bond-slave for life. Scrubbing his filthy clothes, butchering his livestock, bearing his brood of children.

"I won't, I won't," I whispered. I would not submit to either the rifle's ball or a life of endless miserable toil.

So on we went, up and down and over and around.

Then in the distance I saw a low, throbbing light. I smelt smoke and heard a muffled howl. And I thought, They've chased me to the very gates of Satan's realm. But a legion of hissing, leering devils no more frightened me than the thought of returning to the Barrows.

I led on, pulling Brother Boy by the hand. I would rather march into fire than bear the brothers' foul looks another day. But the howl was by one of the pigs, not a damned soul. And the smoky red light was not a glimpse of hellfire but one of my pa's charcoal ricks. We'd fled for miles and come to Pa's outermost fire yard.

Brother Boy had led me all the way home. Yet seeing the heaps of earth with the smoke oozing out gave me no comfort at all. This was home indeed, but home was a ruin, a burnt wasteland.

The closest fire rick had a big crevasse down one side, like a pulsing red wound. I went to the crack, as close as I dared. Inside was smolder and boiling smoke. Shaking with fear and exhaustion, I thought, If only I could go in there, escape to a place where no one would follow.

"He should be around here somewheres," Brother Boy said. I was barely listening, tho. "I saw him here cutting wood the day before. Tending the fires."

Then a great form loomed up to one side of the rick, Leon or Noel, I couldn't tell which. The shadows writhed around him. Smoke seemed to issue from his nose as tho he were burning inside.

Behind us came a grunt and a snarl. The pigs, I thought, come to fight one last battle. Come to save us. But no, it was the other brother.

Leon aimed the rifle at me. His brother shouted a curse and threw a rock to spoil his aim. Noel ran to his brother, grabbing for the rifle. "We should put her down right now like a thieving wolf," Leon said. For a moment, he lowered the gun.

A rag was tied around his head, stained red around his ear. As he came closer, I saw that around his eye was an ugly purple-black bruise. He groaned low and long. I heard pain in the sound, and rage. He fixed me with a black vengeful look.

They must have seen Brother Boy, for he stood right next to me. Yet he seemed invisible to them. He spoke, and they appeared to hear nothing. "She's not your slave," he said. "She's nobody's slave no more."

Noel took up a stout stick and thrust the end into the fiery crack. In a moment it was ablaze, and he held it out for a torch. I saw then that there was a swollen place on his forehead, and toothmarks. But I knew if a pig had gotten a bite at him, it would have torn away a great mouthful. Those marks were made by a man, not a beast.

And his brother's bandage, I saw, was not fresh. It had been there a day or two. On Leon's arm was a long cut, barely healed. And I saw, as he came closer, that he limped.

Again, Brother Boy spoke. "She's not going back with you." He came between me and his brothers. But they saw him not.

"You're a devil," Leon said. "Look what you made us do." He pointed to the side of his head where a mass of hair had been torn out. "Fighting and swearing and plotting against each other. We brought you into our house, and you set us against each other. A witch, that's what you are. And a witch is for hanging. Then for burning."

"She can be tamed," Noel said, trying to calm his brother.

As tho I were a wild and terrible beast, Noel came at me with the torch. His brother approached too, but warily, the rifle's barrel pointed again at my heart.

Leon snarled at me like a mad dog. "You cursed us both, bringing strife and discord into our house."

"I cursed nobody ever in my life," I said plainly. "You cursed yourself."

He aimed direct at my head. The rifle muzzle moved back

and forth, as tho he were pointing first at one eye, and then the other.

"She beguiled you with those evil eyes," Leon said to his brother.

Noel slapped the rifle away, telling him to wait. "I'm the one who decides."

"She'll poison your mind. If she lives, we'll never be happy no more."

"You shut your mouth now. I don't want to hear another word. I decide. I take the girl as a wife if I please. You got no choice."

Leon swore and jabbed the air with his rifle. "She should be hanged for what she done to us. The whole time fighting, making plans to undo each other. She's a serpent, with poison in her bite."

"Shut it!" Noel shouted. "Shut it or I'll whip you like a misbegotten brat."

I saw that right then Leon gave up. With no hope of making their lives the way they were before they knew me, Leon wanted only one thing now. He didn't say another word, but the look on his face told of the hatred in his heart. "You must die for what you've done," his eyes said to me. His were ordinary, not mismatched like mine. But there was death in them, a curse of murder in the way they fixed on me.

While his brother pondered, Leon acted. He raised the rifle. He sighted and pulled the trigger. The shot broke the silence as a hammer would break a looking glass.

I felt the ball graze past my ear. Brother Boy had seen Leon's intention and shouted just as Leon fired. Noel swung his great fist at Leon, knocking him to the ground. He kicked him hard, then grabbed for the rifle. They went at each other, rolling in the dirt. They struggled terrible, with snarls and curses and groans as deep as thunder.

Finally, Noel gave his brother a fist to the side of his head and the fight was over. Leon lay there rubbing his jaw and murmuring curses. Noel scrambled backward and got to his feet. "She's mine," he growled. "Mine."

He turned to me. "I still own you," he said. "I can do as I like with you. I got a contract signed and sealed."

"Nobody owns me," I said. Quiet, low almost to a whisper, but they all heard me. "No one ever did nor ever will. Not you brothers and not even my own pa."

"He sold you off, girl. You're mine."

"Here's your contract." These words came from nowhere, from the darkness. "Set her free." It was my pa, speaking but unseen. "We can make the contract null right here and now."

Why couldn't I see him? Was I bereft of my senses? Or was he dead and gone and speaking from the next world? Revenging ghost or guardian angel, he might have been either, or both at the same time.

"Say it now: the agreement is broken. Give me back my daughter and you'll have your money."

Then I saw him. He was panting heavy from running. He came at the brothers with a scroll of paper in one hand.

"Here's your contract. One year of servitude for a hundred dollars. I'll buy her back, and you'll be free of her forever."

"I paid you cash money."

"You'll have your money," Pa said coming into the torch light. "I'll sell off another dozen acres tomorrow to raise it." He was different now from the last time I saw him. The madness was no longer in his eyes. He'd found no treasure. He'd gone back to his hard labors of cutting wood and burning it for charcoal. The cloud of treasure-hunting greed had passed. He'd lost me and finally understood that he needed me back. "I'll pledge over twelve acres of fine land to fulfill the contract. You'll have your profit, and you'll be free of what you call a curse."

"I'm no curse," I said, louder now. "If these two dispute and plot and fight, that's because the vicious thoughts are already there. I didn't do a thing but work."

Leon leaned against a tree, cradling the rifle. He held up his hand to show a blood black twisted finger. "My own brother did this," he snarled. "And last night I almost slit his throat as he slept. The girl's a witch with those evil eyes, and she put us under a spell. I come out alone tonight to hunt the witch girl down and kill her. For she's put a curse on me, on my brother, on us both. But Noel heard me get up. He followed."

"Then put your names to the contract to say it's broken," Pa said, "and you'll never see her again."

"Nor never see me," Brother Boy said. They heard. They

must have. But they pretended there was only silence. "Never see me!" he shouted. Still they pondered.

"She can be broken," Noel said, more to himself than to anyone listening. "I was just too easy on her. Too much sweet talk and not enough hard work. I still got a legal claim to her."

"But you don't really want her," Pa said. I'd never heard his voice that way. There was a tremble in it, as tho he finally had woken up and seen what was real. "She's no good to you. You don't want her. Not truly. You don't need her." There came a long silence. "But I do."

"I have a claim," Noel said.

"I told you I'd pay it in full. You can get along without her. I cannot. Truly, she's all I've got left in the world." He wasn't begging. He still had his dignity. But it was clear to them, to me, how true his words were.

Leon was fumbling there in the dark. I saw the glint of the rifle barrel as he lifted it one last time. While his brother parlayed with my pa, Leon was reloading.

The trigger clicked. The hammer came down. But that was all. He tried again, aiming with shaky arms at his brother.

Noel grabbed it from him and heaved it out into the bush.

Then cursing me, cursing my pa, cursing his brother and the whole world, Noel took the contract out of Pa's hands. He didn't look at the words, not even a glance. He just snarled like a bear caught in an iron trap and jammed the paper into the fire hole. It caught fire and blazed and was gone. And with that, they were free of me and I of them.

He helped his brother get up. They didn't look back. They didn't say another word. Together they stalked off into the forest shadows.

A puff of breath from inside the coal rick blew the burnt contract out and upward. It circled, then was drawn higher and disappeared like a bat flittering into the upper darkness.

Chapter 42

WE WENT BACK TO OUR CABIN. BROTHER BOY CAME too. Pa didn't say much, but I knew he was happy that I was back under his roof.

After we ate, I went to my loft, to my old bed. Brother Boy stayed the day, sleeping too, in Pa's bed downstairs.

I heard rain on the roof in the afternoon and drowsed in and out, listening to the drumming storm music. When I was roused to full waking, I climbed down the ladder and found my pa and Brother Boy sitting before a low fire. "There's johnnycakes there," Pa said.

"And venison meat," Brother Boy added.

He'd gone back to his den while I slept. Along with the meat and a jug of cider, he'd gotten the great ivory tusk. Now Pa was examining it, turning it round and round and muttering happily.

"Treasure," he said. "This is the treasure I sought." We

didn't tell Brother Boy that it was off a great beast from the ancient times.

"You can sell it," Brother Boy said. "It's yours now. I got no use for it. You and One Green Eye can sell it for cash money."

"But you found it," Pa said, shaking his head. "It's yours to sell as you please, not ours."

Brother Boy shrugged. "It's my present. Take it. I got nothing else to give."

And that's how we bought back the best acres Pa had lost. He could be foolish at times, but Pa knew wherefore and when and how much for such things. He wrote letters back and forth with the man who had a museum of curiosities. He was sure the man would pay a hefty sum to own the tusk, place it on display, and charge folks to see such a marvel. So Pa found his treasure, and I found my true friend. And not even six months later, Noel and Leon sold their whole property to a family from the Mohawk Valley and moved out to better land in the Ohio territory. And they were heard of never again.

Chapter 43

BROTHER BOY CAME OUT TO VISIT US SOME NIGHTS. He liked to hear Pa talk about his strange books and the men who put all those words down. But the pictures were his favorite part. Some showed beasts from far-off lands, lions and elephants and the great African monkeys who look like hairy men. Others showed the faces of kings and queens. He liked to hear Pa read their names and all the wonderful things they did.

One night he saw the glimmer of firelight in my little looking glass. There was the flame in the hearth, and there was its twin flickering on the shiny silver pane. He picked up the glass and held it so he could see himself close and clear.

I watched him watching himself. And I almost had to look away, for it was like something too private to witness. He stared and stared. And it finally came to me: he's never really seen himself. Perhaps he'd had a glimpse in a still pool of water, but for all the years he'd lived alone, there had been no looking glass. And I hadn't seen one either at the Barrows' house. His own face was strange to him.

I took out the wash water to dump. I wrapped what was left of the cheese in oil cloth and took it down to the spring house to keep cool. When I got back, he was still looking in the glass. But he turned and stared at me, as tho he might see himself in my face.

I remembered as a little girl looking up into Pa's face as if it were a glass. If he was smiling, then I was a good girl, or a pretty girl, or a hardworking girl. If he was scowling, then I was terrible and ugly.

Now Brother Boy regarded me with the same kind of unsaid question. I nodded and smiled. I looked him eye to eye as if to tell him with no words that he was not just my good friend but worthy too.

Then, satisfied, he put the glass back where he'd found it.

Chapter 44

I SAW THE NORTHERN LIGHTS ONE MORE TIME THAT year. I went out to visit Brother Boy in his den. I'd brought food for supper and stayed late teaching him a little more how to read, as he had asked me to do. By the end of the summer, he'd learned all the letters of his name and would practice them on a piece of slate.

"*B* for *Brother Boy*," he said, proud as a prize rooster. "*O* for *one*, and *y* for *you*." It was like with every letter of his name that he mastered, he was a little more real. He looked to me as he recited "*B. O. Y.*"

I nodded and said, "Yes, that's right." But I didn't need to talk. He could see the yes in my eyes.

It was terrible dark when I left his little house and started for home. But I'd gone enough times to know the path. And there was nothing to fear between his home and mine.

I went a ways down the path, when I heard Brother Boy coming to catch up with me. "Hey!" he called out. "Wait for me!"

"You want to stay with me and Pa tonight?"

"No. I just want to see the lights. I got a feeling they'll be out."

So we climbed the hilltop where we'd seen the lights before. We waited awhile, the two of us, quiet and peaceful. Maybe it was the right time of night, or maybe the proper season. But they did indeed come, churning and quaking and more beautiful than any sight I'd seen.

"Sometimes," I said, "I think about going up with all those spirits who are riding the bright tide in the sky. I consider on how joysome it would be to rise on a night like this to Heaven."

I looked up at the lights with one eye closed. Then I tried the other. On the right, they were bright and pure like colors nobody had ever seen before. On the left they were more hazy, softer and dreamlike. It was different, one side and then the other. And yet it was the same.

"You're not really thinking of going off, are you?" Brother Boy asked.

"No, that's just a dream. I got Pa to take care of, and I got you to be my friend. I'm not going to leave either of you."

"Good," he said, soft, the way you might say "amen" at the end of a prayer.

And we stayed out there on the hilltop together until the lights had all faded.